The BOOBY TRAP and other Bits and Boobs

The BOOBY TRAP and other Bits and Boobs

Edited by DAWN O'PORTER

HOT KEY BOOKS

First published in Great Britain in 2013 by Hot Key Books
Northburgh House, 10 Northburgh Street, London EC1V 0AT

A CIP catalogue record for this book is available from the British Library.

Paperback ISBN: 978-1-4714-0142-8
Export ISBN: 978-1-4714-0144-2
1

This book is typeset in 10.5 Berling LT Std using Atomik ePublisher

Printed and bound by Clays Ltd, St Ives Plc

Hot Key Books supports the Forest Stewardship Council (FSC),
the leading international forest certification organisation, and is committed to
printing only on Greenpeace-approved FSC-certified paper.

www.hotkeybooks.com

Hot Key Books is part of the Bonnier Publishing Group
www.bonnierpublishing.com

Dedicated to . . . jugs, baps, tits, bangers, knorks, melons, airbags, Jedwards, funbags, flop-a-dops, over-the-shoulder boulder-holders, bozangers, wangers, jubblies, boobies, waps, Phil and Grant, Golden Globes, hooters, the Girls, cans, mollies, babylons, nip nips, chesticles, bazookas, Bristols . . .

Contents

INTRODUCTION BY DAWN O'PORTER

I am obsessed with tits.

I stare at them – I can't help it. I am the woman you catch glaring at your nipples in the gym changing room, and I find it almost impossible not to pass comment on a pair that I find attractive. It's a perversion that I don't bother trying to hide. Most of my female friends will tell you that I sneak a peek whenever I can. Skype me and I will flash you, then probably ask to be flashed back. Get changed at my house? Expect to be gawked at. I can't help it. I just love them. Tits. BRRRRRRRR.

As well as my appreciation for the way they look, their function blows my mind. Having watched my sister's children suckle from them and grow, I understand the value of their power. But I only have to let down the guard of my subconscious for a millionth of a second to have my mind flurried with reminders that those fountains of life may also be the source of death. It's a negative connotation I have learned to suppress enough for my love of boobs to be a true pleasure in my life, but it's always there somewhere. I was six years old (two days off seven) when my mother died of breast cancer, on 21st January 1986. I am still full of questions about who my mother was,

1

and why it happened. Everything I am stems from a fear of abandonment or the fear of history repeating itself, and at the age of thirty-four I can cry on demand if I dare think back to being six years old.

And now, still, boobs are scarcely off my mind. So off the back of the obsession I give you: *The Booby Trap and Other Bits and Boobs*. An entire book about boobs. You. Are. Welcome!

What you are about to read is a vibrant mix of fact and fiction, prose and poetry. We have drawings too – even a photo of a feminist's torso! When my publishers, Hot Key Books, gave the go ahead for this book, the brief was simple: 'Get as many famous people as you can to write whatever they like about anything to do with boobs at any point in their life.' So that's what I did – I shamelessly approached everyone I had access to, and the result makes for brilliant reading.

What makes this even better is that proceeds from the sales of this book will be split between my three favourite breast cancer charities. I couldn't decide which one of them to pick so I picked them all. We have Breast Cancer Care, Breakthrough Breast Cancer and CoppaFeel! So that's care, research and awareness all covered. At the back of the book you can find out a bit more about what each charity does along with all of their contact details.

The thing about breast cancer is that if you catch it early, the chances of you being absolutely fine are very very high. Most breast cancers are found by self-examination, so before you start reading, please put down this book, lift up your top, and have a good feel of your boobs. Also at the back of the book is a step-by-step guide on how to check your boobs properly.

Make it part of your routine, get to know how they feel so you know if anything changes. Who said groping couldn't save lives? Done? Great, let's crack on . . .

I Am Fifteen, and Have Nothing Figured Out

MAUDE APATOW

I often wonder why I am so full of rage. I like to blame it on my boobs. I have always been mad at my boobs. When I was ten my aunt had just finished chemotherapy and my grandmother was dying of cancer. I didn't have boobs then, but I already hated them because all I knew about them was that they fed babies and hurt people.

When I got boobs, I was ashamed of them and hid them. They also kind of grossed me out and I thought they made me look deformed. The first memories I have about my boobs are how I would constantly run into things and how it would hurt so badly that I would cry. I would also cry because it was like life was never going to be the same. In fourth grade, I was very nostalgic and emotional.

I used to think if I lay down on the marble floor, face down, maybe they would go away. I also liked the pain. I made myself cry, but I didn't get up. I was so confused, I decided to torture myself. After doing that a few times, I was afraid they would pop or crack open (a horrifying thought) and stopped. That was when I first started getting nervous. I wish I could say that I'm over this and laugh at how at how neurotic and strange I was, but I am not any less confused now.

I feel like by sixth grade, mostly everyone had boobs, but it was hard to tell because a majority of my friends would hide them with baggy T-shirts. I invited four girls to sleep over at my house at the end of sixth grade. They were a lot more mature and comfortable with themselves than I was (and still am). I like to have more than one person at my house because I'm easily overwhelmed and offended, and so I could leave if I wanted to and it wouldn't be as weird (still a little weird though). We watched the film *Cabaret*, which, I think, is what inspired the events that followed. I had only met these girls a couple of months prior to this night, so I was not comfortable with them at all (that has not changed). After the movie ended we were all in the room and a few minutes later, everyone was topless. I was not. They all started to yell at me to take off my shirt, but I said no. Then they cornered me and locked me in the bathroom with them. I closed my eyes because I didn't need to see that. I felt their boobs touching my face and shoulders. They laughed and thought it was hilarious. It scarred me.

In middle school my friend had a crush on her neighbor. She kept track of the days he would go on jogs and on those days she would stand by her window and flash him. The details are sketchy and we aren't sure if he ever even saw. I remember this enraged me. I told my parents right away because no one in my grade thought there was anything wrong with it.

There was a Bar or Bat Mitzvah almost every weekend in seventh grade. Thirteen-year-old girls would wear super-tight black dresses and five-inch heels and that appalled me. This is probably when I separated from my friends and became more like a mom. I would yell at everyone to stop texting during the services, because I didn't understand how someone could do something so disrespectful. I think I did this because it gave me something to do (not sure why that was fun for me, it only caused pain). I remember sitting behind a group of girls, so I could get a good look to see if they were on their phones or not, and noticing that they had their bras tightened all the way. The clasp was all the way up their backs. I later noticed that they were pushing their tween boobs up so high, it looked painful. I used to think that I was the strange one for not wanting to do that to myself, but now I know I wasn't.

I'm afraid to show people my boobs. There is a chance they look really weird and I don't know it – or no one has told me before. I'm pretty sure they're normal but I don't want to risk it. I am so charged with hormones, I can't handle any type of comment that would make me feel bad.

My mom always tells me to show my boobs off now, because they will never look this good again. That makes me feel terrible and sad because thinking about aging makes me feel depressed.

My best friend is a 34DD, so it is hard to avoid the boob topic.

I'm fifteen and I am still trying to understand why people my age do certain things, like why a girl would send a picture of their boobs to a boy and not expect everyone in the school to see it. Is she really that confused and careless or is it a cry for help and attention? I feel alone in the sense that not many people my age care about people as deeply as I do. I get worked up and upset about things that other people don't even think about. I didn't think about why girls were wearing such padded bras at twelve and thirteen and how it says something about who you are. Right now I am trying to figure out what that is. Experimenting comes with getting older. I know that there is nothing I can do to stop my friends from trying things like drinking or drugs, but it is really hard to accept that. I have always been anxious and have felt like I need to control what everyone around me is doing. I figured out that the reason I try to protect people is because I am trying to protect myself. I don't want to help my friends through things I feel like I could have prevented. I know that I don't have control and that I really can't prevent bad things from happening, but I still feel worried. My friends have isolated me because I don't support them and it feels terrible. As soon as boobs come, everyone wants to grow up. To me, boobs symbolize change, growth, puberty, and the reason all of my friends and I all went crazy. Maybe if my grandma didn't die so young, I wouldn't be so freaked out that bad things would happen to everyone all of the time. I haven't had a baby or a boyfriend yet, so I don't know any of the positive reasons to have boobs. All I know is I hit them on doorways sometimes and it really hurts.

EDITH BOWMAN

You are a thing of wonder, both in the vein of intrigue and amusement. From the very start you set out to have a mind of your own, changing and developing at your own pace, binded to each other but at the same time occasionally estranged.

I remember way back then, when you started to grow. I was the subject of ridicule from others who presumed it was all premature on my part. Who was I to think that I needed to support you, help you evolve! I felt shame and confusion.

Even now as I sit here in between relying on you to provide nourishment for my newborn I can feel you tingle, regale and prepare. You give, you fatten, you strengthen, you comfort and you leak.

And yet you also take, you allow life to be devoured by an evil poison. A poison that threatened to take away the very person who has chaperoned our relationship from the start. You were the reason I nearly lost my mum. Mistrust between us that I hope will never reappear.

Then there is your seductive side, affirming powers of flirtation, feeling sexy, provocative and womanly. Something to thank you for and something I never want to lose.

Onwards we go on this journey together, a journey that neither of us can predict nor regulate, but one that I know will continue to test both our very existences.

AMANDA BYRAM

Boobies, mammaries, mams, titties, tits, Bill and Ben, puppies, the Girls, whammers, knockers, breasticulars, boobage, bazookas, cleavefest. Somehow it seems our most prized possessions are always void of a moniker with class. So many silly words to describe our precious bumps! Yet the truth is, as much as we moan about them, they are our most treasured assets.

The story of the life of my 'Girls' starts quite late. I was thirteen and the only girl left in my class with a pink vest complete with ribbon at the chest, just where my cleavage should have been. But alas, cleavage would have to wait. I was flatter than a pancake.

Being the only girl in my year without a training bra was fast becoming an issue for my thirteen-year-old self, especially in the changing room after P.E. class, so I decided to take matters into my own hands. I snuck into my big sister's underwear drawer and – gasp – stole a bra. I wore this little sucker 24/7 for a year, only undoing the back clasp when I went to kiss my parents goodnight, so they wouldn't feel it when they hugged me. I was a bra ninja. Stealth and cunning.

Post-ninja years, I became a model. I had outgrown my feeble training bra with gusto and blossomed a great big handful of boobage. I was commonly known as 'Boobs Byram: the Best in the Biz' (true story).

Then unfortunately, like with most young girls, along came dieting. Diets 'boob-napped' my precious puppies in one fell cup of lettuce leaves. Much to my disappointment I never regained full possession of those bouncy eager breasts ever again.

And now, with age they have settled. Settled for a life of comfort, just hanging around. 'The Mams' and I have been through quite a lot together. They are always there for me, and with me, every day. They are neither big nor small now, but I love them unconditionally. And they will always be mine.

MELANIE C

I've always had a strange relationship with my boobs, ever since those difficult puberty years. I remember the first girl at school to get them, everyone else sprouting and moving out of vests into 'training' bras, and eventually persuading my mum to get me one when I really didn't need one! 'Nature is cruel,' I thought. 'Maybe I'll wake up with big bazookas one morning?' I never did. Being a sporty type I've always had an athletic build, and no amount of padding, toilet tissue or chicken fillets could create a cleavage. That was until I got pregnant, and then . . . boom! Hello, boobies!

This was when everything changed – not only with my boobs but my whole body. Having a new life growing inside me was miraculous and liberating. I suddenly saw my body as an incredible, magical machine.

When I had my little girl I was lucky enough to be able to breastfeed. It was an amazing experience, incredibly painful and frustrating at times, but I felt like my newborn was teaching me what to do. I forgave nature. What an incredible thing! My boobs helped me nourish and nurture a healthy and wonderful child. I couldn't be more proud of them!

AMANDA DE CADENET

My boobs . . . I've said those words so many times.

My boobs have been talked about for so long they are almost more famous than me.

I understand why – they are a great pair, despite breastfeeding three kids. You can't ignore them, and I'm OK with that. I must say that having larger boobs – mine are currently 38DD – can be a real distraction, though more to other people than to me. It's not like I sit around thinking about them or fondling them, but more when I try a new bikini on and realise I need a size 12 for my bum and a size 16 for my boobs. I am sorry to say it, but I have swapped sizes out on the rack many times to accommodate my ample breasts.

In all seriousness, I know enough about breast health that I went for my first mammogram last year, even though I was told I'm 'too young' to worry. I wasn't worried – I just want to be safe. I went with a girlfriend, and we made a day of it, had some food, a catch-up and went in to get our boobs squashed in the mammogram machine. Much more fun to do it in the room with a pal – I highly recommend it.

I figure that it's my job to take care of these precious beauties, even though some days I don't speak nicely to them, like when none of my bras fit or they go up a whole size when my period arrives. But, let's face it, even though I would fit into dresses that have otherwise evaded me and people would look at my face when I walked into the room instead of my tits, I just wouldn't be me without these breasts, and I am learning to love them a day at a time.

GEMMA CAIRNEY

I'm not really sure how to tell this. But once my boyfriend accidentally bit my nipple really, really hard. It was a memorably painful moment, though done with nothing but love. Weird and embarrassing, but true. One day it may happen to you.

The NBB

Beware of the NBB.
When the feeling is right
On red a red-light night
It'll be his penchant for bazongas
His sheer enthusiasm for areola
Tit-allation, is his adoration.
It can sometimes get the better of him, like when you take
the first bite of a strawberry lace
The NBB gets giddy (at occasionally an alarming pace)
Beware of the NBB
O just how he loves to feast
That Nipple Biting Beast.

SARA COX

In the middle of a neatly trimmed lawn in the north-west of England stands a small tent. Inside the tent, four eleven-year-old girls huddle closely together, mainly because it's not a very spacious tent, but also because one of the Joannes (whose lawn they are currently sitting on) is about to unveil something magnificent: her first bra. It is a size AAA training bra in pristine white. The girls' gasps of admiration can easily be heard through the flimsy canvas as Joanne whips up her top. The other Joanne, Lisa and the young me glance at each other enviously.

Joanne-with-the-bra was that kind of girl. Long blonde wavy hair, almond-shaped eyes. She was a success. Unlike myself at that age, her knees weren't wider than her thighs and her forehead wasn't big enough to double up as a five-a-side pitch. In the great netball game of life, she was the centre to my goalkeeper. And now she'd beaten me to boobs as well, and with it, a training bra. Quite a curious name for what was essentially a crop top; what would these bras train your fledgling boobs to do? Jump through hoops? Of course as all girls eventually learn, the only tits jumping through hoops would be boys desperate to shove a hand up your Aran number for a squeeze of your jumper bumps.

I had no such concerns as a pre-teen, as I had no jumper bumps. I didn't even have a ripple. I was so flat-chested well into my teenage years that the boys at school composed a special remix of the theme tune to the popular sci-fi cartoon *Ulysses*, altering the lyrics to reflect my lack of boobage, resulting in 'Vertices, vertices, floating through all the galaxies' being sung at volume into my face.

As my friends blossomed around me, blooming into womanly shapes, I remained twig-like. If I'd had the chance to hook up with Zoltar, like Tom Hanks in *Big*, my wish wouldn't have been to be big, but to be booby, which I suppose would've made for a different kind of movie all together.

My prayers to Norksella, the goddess of breasts, were answered abruptly around my fifteenth birthday. It's as if Mother Nature had totally forgotten about me so gave me double helpings to compensate.

Now, after so much yearning, I found myself with quite sizeable funbags, which over the years have been varying degrees of fun. I could suddenly get into clubs and bars as doormen were too mesmerised by my DDs to worry about my ID.

During my illustrious modelling career I was sent to South Korea as 'Your chest is too big for Tokyo', like my wabs were Godzilla and could overrun the city.

Pregnancies saw them inflate to the size of two Smart cars and breastfeeding was almost impossible.

They've been pushed up, flattened down, hoisted skywards and sometimes I've woken up to find one under my armpit and the other over my shoulder, but they're my boobs and I've grown to love them.

I guess the moral of this tale is be careful what you wish for, 'cos if you get it, bikini shopping is a bugger.

Diary of a Boob Job

JAMES DAWSON

1 DAY PRE-OP

Hi everyone, my name is Becca Hayes. I'm twenty years old and I live in South London. I work in recruitment but that's really boring, you don't need to know about that. Basically, the thing is, I'm having a boob job – a breast enlargement – tomorrow, and I thought it'd be really good for all you ladies out there, who are thinking about having one, to blog about it. I know when I was researching the op, I had, like, a million questions, so I hope this is helpful!

OK, here goes! Writing this is good because it's taking my mind off tomorrow morning. I'm not gonna lie, I'm properly shitting myself. Seriously, my hands are actually shaking while I type. I feel really sick, but that might be because I've not had anything to eat since lunch – I have to be nil-by-mouth for tomorrow. Leaving a Kinder Bueno in the fridge was a big mistake HA!

I was really excited up until about ten minutes ago and then reality sort of sunk in. We had a girls' night tonight – some of my mates came round and I suppose we sort of had a boob party! I've done my nails, I've had my tan, I got my hair dyed – basically I want everything to be perfect for tomorrow. I want to wake up, stick my lashes on and be like 'Ta-da! Check 'em out!' But now everyone's gone I'm freaking out! I don't like it!

Deep breaths! So here's the technical stuff. I'm getting 250cc silicone implants inserted under the muscle. I saw a couple of doctors and they both said I shouldn't really go a lot bigger because I'm only little – five two and quite skinny. Obviously I want the girls to be bigger, but I don't want to look like a Barbie doll either. I went for silicone over saline just because my doctor said they'd be safer . . . apparently the newer implants *can't* leak, which is what freaks me out the most. I don't know about you, but I've seen those documentaries where the silicone leaks into the rest of the body and there're lumps and bumps and black shit everywhere. My doctor said that that just *can't* happen anymore.

Right now it's about midnight. I'm in bed, but there's no way I'm gonna sleep. I'm wide awake. I would literally kill for a cup of tea, but I'm not allowed. We have to leave here at six thirty to get to the hospital – I live with my sister, so she's taken the day off work to come with me. She's fast asleep in the next room. I might honestly just stay awake all night; I'll probably be less tired – you know like when you pull an all-nighter on a random Thursday out and then power through to the office Friday morning.

I AM BRICKING IT.

At my consultation they made me sign one of those 'if you die during this operation it's your own stupid fault' forms – like a disclaimer or whatever they're called. Some people go under the anaesthetic and just don't wake up. I must be mad. I actually paid for this.

Ooh, that's a good point actually. How much did I pay? I had no idea about how much these things cost until I went to my first appointment. Personally, I'm paying six grand for the op. I love how my doctor explained it was three grand per boob. Like who's gonna get just one done, right?

I decided to take out a loan in the end because to save up six grand would have taken *forever*. I had like two thousand pounds saved already but borrowed the rest. I'll be paying for these puppies for about five years, but I really think it's gonna be worth it. At the moment, I'm just trying to forget about what the next six weeks are going to be like and just focus on how amazing it'll be to have perfect boobs.

I could have saved a shitload of money by going abroad to get them done. Seriously, even with flights and hotels and stuff it would have been cheaper to go to Belgium or somewhere. But I was worried that the hospital would be like something out of *Hostel* though, and I wanted to be near my mum in case something goes wrong. A friend of my mate Abbie went to South Africa for lipo and when she got an infection it ended up costing twice as much to get the aftercare back home, so I was like SOD THAT. Like you get what you pay for.

I suppose I should describe what they're like now really. I'll upload some 'before' pics, obviously. I call them Mary-Kate and Ashley cos they're my twins! Bless 'em, but they're tiny.

I mean like teeny-tiny, right? At the moment I'm a 32AA and I'm *hoping* to go up to a C cup. It's a bit bollocks, but the doctors can't promise what *size* they'll be after the op because they only work with the size of the implant. I won't actually know what bra size I'll need until a few weeks after the op, which is slightly worrying.

So why am I getting it done? I'm definitely getting it done for me. I'm young, I'm single, I've got a job, so why not? My mum and sister think I'm mental, but they don't have boy chests. People always say 'look at models, they never have boobs' – yeah, well, they're also six foot tall and *models*. I am clearly not a model. I suppose, as much as I love Mary-Kate and Ashley, I just wanna feel more womanly and curvy.

I remember the first girl in our year to get boobs. I think it was Year Five and Jenny Pullman – I think she died last year so I shouldn't be shady – just ballooned overnight. We could all see the outline of her training bra through her yellow blouse – the boys were mesmerised, and us girls were all desperate to see them when we got changed for PE! I couldn't wait for mine to pop out too. Well, I'm still waiting! I don't know about you, but when I was little – well, like twelve or thirteen – I used to lie in bed and actually pray that tomorrow would be the day I woke up with big breasts. We never even went to church, but I used to properly put my hands together and pray to the God of Boobs. Obviously it didn't work.

When I go out with my mate Cherise, she's (and I'm not being a bitch cos she looks great) quite a lot bigger than me, but she always gets all the attention from the lads. Take last Friday night for example – we went out near Clapham

Junction to this amazing tiki bar place that's done up to look like a grotto. Me and Claire, my sister, got there first and were already at the bar when Cherise walked in. I swear time stopped, the music went quiet and every ~~penis~~ pair of eyes in the bar followed her across the room like she was the Pied bloody Piper or something.

She didn't even have her boobs on display or nothing – they're just *there* – but within about thirty seconds flat, some preppy city boy in one of them candy-stripe shirts was offering to buy her a Woo-Woo. I might as well have been invisible. I reckon having an amazing rack means she just has more confidence, like a glow or something. Whatever it is, I want a piece of that. I'm bloody sick to the back teeth of worrying about my chest.

Every single time I've been with a guy (and no, I'm not gonna put my magic number on here!) I *dread* getting my kit off. The terror starts as soon as you have a snog. Picture the scene. You've been on a date or out dancing and he comes back to yours. You stick Adele on and get a glass of wine. You move to the sofa and make some chit-chat before he goes in for the kill. You know how it goes, the kiss gets deeper and his hands start wandering . . .

That's when I stop thinking about the kiss and one thought fills my head . . . CHICKEN FILLETS. You can feel it in the way the kiss changes rhythm – he *knows*. He's wondering if he can sue for false advertising. All I can think about is how I'm gonna whip them out without him noticing or about how I'm going to have to apologise for the major lack of breasts. You can see it though, even though they all say it's not a problem.

They smile, but they don't smile with their eyes. *Gutted. Flat as a pancake.*

Anyway, never mind the guys. This is a present to myself. I'm gonna feel better with bigger boobs. You've gotta love yourself, right?!

This wasn't an impulse buy, girls. It's not like I was at the checkout at Tesco and suddenly thought, 'Ooh, maybe I'll get some chewing gum and some silicone implants.' I've been wanting this since I was about fifteen when I finally realised they weren't gonna appear overnight. I am fully, a hundred per cent sure I want this, but tonight the nerves have set in because it's *real* now. Tomorrow I'm finally getting some boobs.

I guess I should *try* to get some sleep now or tomorrow I'm gonna feel like total shit. I'll take my laptop to the hospital so I'll blog as soon as I can after the op. I don't know how long that's gonna be, cos I'm gonna be really out of it. What I'll do is, I'll show you what it looks like afterwards (probably be a bit of a car crash, but hey-ho) and then again a few weeks later when all the bandages are off and you can compare before and after.

For now though, if you've got any questions, leave them in the comments box.

Becca xxx

DAY OF THE OP

OK, I'm typing in italics because I'm WHISPERING! I don't even think I'm meant to be using my laptop, but I'm waiting to go in now. I've been waiting for like an hour and I'm by myself AND I accidentally left my magazine in Claire's bag!!!

I wish I could share how sexy I look right now. I'm naked except for a shitty blue nightie thing. My bum is hanging out where it's tied at the back! About an hour ago, the surgeon came to mark me up: There's lines all over my chest where he's gonna cut me. They go underneath the girls and diagonally across where the muscle is apparently. I look like a frigging dot-to-dot drawing.

I had to send Claire out. The look on her face was freaking me out and every time I tried to speak to her it felt like I might throw up. I wonder if that's why they don't let you eat.

Right up until we got to the hospital I seriously thought I might back out. In the car I looked at Claire and was about a second away from telling her to turn around, but then I was like 'no, you've paid for it, you're doing it'. I think I've come too far now. I suppose I don't HAVE to go through with it, but I'd look properly mental if I freaked out now. I wish I wasn't by myself. I was OK when Si was here – he's the surgeon – South African guy. He'd be quite hot if he wasn't bald. Now he's gone I don't know if I can go through with it.

I just have to keep thinking about what they'll be like in six weeks. I've got this image of me and the new boobs walking down the road wearing a really nice top – nothing tarty – and just feeling like I'm floating in slow motion; all the boys looking back at me. I've got to keep that in my head.

This is so much harder than I thought it was gonna be.

OK. The nurse has just been in to tell me I'm next. Here we go.

TEN DAYS AFTER OP

Hey everyone! Thank you so much for all your comments and get-well-soon messages! They really cheered me up loads. I can't believe how many people have read the last post and I'm so sorry I didn't update the blog sooner.

I'm not gonna lie, I've been feeling pretty shit. I still feel shit, but a lot less shit than I was. I'm high as a kite on codeine but I'll do my best to run you through everything that happened.

So I went into get my anaesthetic and I was really worried about waking up halfway through the op, but anaesthetist lady said that wasn't gonna happen. Next thing I knew I was awake and freaking out in the recovery room. I got really pissed off with the nurse because I thought if I didn't go find Claire she'd leave without me. I was pretty out of it!

I can't explain how weird it felt. It really did feel like there was a huge fat guy sat on my chest – that's how heavy they felt. It was crushing at first.

Anyway, turns out Claire realised we hadn't brought a sports bra – we'd both completely forgotten – so she'd done a dash to M&S for me. I've been stuck in the bastard thing ever since.

To be honest, the pain hasn't been as bad as I thought, but I am off my tits (ha) on drugs. Word of warning: I didn't do a poo for like three days. The constipation from all the morphine was maybe the worst part, I was bloated and fat and minging. THEY SHOULD TELL YOU THAT AT THE START! The *pain* though wasn't *that* bad. It's weird. The pain is sort of in my arms and shoulders. Believe me, you will NEED someone to help you around the house. Claire has been amazing helping me get dressed and washed and stuff. All you mums out there, seriously, you will want someone around cos there is *no way* you're lifting a baby.

The worst part, way worse than the pain, is how they looked. They looked fucking awful. Sorry about the language, but they really did. On the first night out of the hospital I cried and cried and cried. They were so high up they were almost on my chin. I was so angry, I really did think the op had gone wrong, but Si kept telling me it was fine and this is what it was like. All I could think was 'all that stress, all that money and pain, and it's GONE WRONG'. No one wants mutant boobs and I was devastated. I made Claire call Si like five times and he said they'd relax and drop over the next few days.

Luckily for him (because I would have actually killed him) they have calmed down. You can tell straight away they're bigger. Like loads bigger. I know they're still swollen, and they will get smaller, but Mary-Kate and Ashley are all grown up! They don't feel as hard as I thought they might and they've settled into more or less the right position. It's hard to tell because I'm still in bandages for another four days, and the stitches still need to come out.

I really do like them. Sorry, I'm finding it really hard to sound pleased or excited because I'm just so fucking tired and sore. I normally roll around in bed but while the gauze is on I have to lie propped up on my back, so I've hardly slept a wink all week. In the end I went to my GP and she gave me a week's supply of sleeping pills. I'm so, SO glad I booked the time off work. At the moment, the only thing I can think about is my boobs. It's insane, but it's like they've become my whole life.

Right now, I just want the bandages off and the stitches out so I can see what they look like and get on with the rest of my life. It's like I had to wait twenty years to get some boobs and now I'm waiting *again*. I'm running out of patience, I just want it over and done with.

Good news is, I've lost weight. Because the painkillers make me feel vommy, I've hardly eaten all week, so that's good, I guess. Sorry I sound so bloody miserable. After I've been for my two-week check-up, I'll show you what they look like and I'm sure they'll be looking great.

TEN WEEKS POST OP

Hey! Sorry it's been so long since my last post. Thanks again for all your comments – I bet you're dying to know how I'm getting on. Well, take a look at the pics! What do you think? Before and after! Pretty different huh? BOOOOOOBS!

You'll note that I am wearing a perfectly normal bra. If I never wear a sports bra ever again it will be too soon. I cannot tell you how amazing it was to go into La Senza and just buy a bra. Not a tiny special-needs mega-padded bra, just a bra. I've bought like a hundred. OK, not a hundred, but more than I need!

I am THRILLED to say that I'm now a 32 C – which is sort of what Si predicted, so I guess he must be pretty good after all! The last time I wrote, I was on a major Debbie Downer, but I just wanted to be able to have a shower and wash my own hair and do normal stuff.

Erm . . . after the last post (just re-reading it!) I went to have the gauze off and get the stitches out – although it actually turned out the stitches were dissolvable so they fell out by themselves. I'm trying to think of stuff you should know . . . I guess I should talk about the scars. Obviously there is some scarring, but you can't really see them unless you look – they're right in the crease under the boob. At first they were hideous like two Joker grins– red and horrid. They've faded though, thank God. I'm using bio-oil on them cos that helps them heal apparently. Claire says she can hardly see them, but I know they're there. I'm really worried that when I lie down guys will see them straight away too.

All that stuff about your nipples dying is bollocks. I can still feel them, thank you very much. Because the implant is under the muscle I should be able to breastfeed too, if I even want kids. The only other thing you've asked a lot of questions about is how long they last. The honest answer is, I don't know. Si didn't seem all that bothered about it when I asked, so I think they last years and years. They do decay though. I get that I'll have to replace them for as long as I want them (and pay all over again), but that's something to worry about further down the line.

As you can see they're looking much better. I have actual cleavage! My mates are pretty jealous. I've never been so groped in my life – everyone wants to cop a feel! They all seem obsessed with them being hard – I don't think *Mean Girls* helped the rep of implants! Basically, at first they looked and felt awful, like I said, but they're MUCH softer now. After much boob squishing, I don't think they're all that different to Cherise's real ones.

Cherise thinks she can tell the difference between real ones and fake ones but I don't think you can unless you get close up and personal. I've road tested them a couple of times in bars and stuff. We went out a week or so after I'd had the dressing off – just around Covent Garden. The difference was insane – for the first time in my life I'm catching guys talking to my chest instead of my face. I honestly don't know if I'm offended or not! It's like, 'My eyes are up here, guys!' It actually makes you a bit paranoid. You don't know if the reason they're staring is because they like what they see or whether they're trying to work out if they're fake. I mean, I *don't* think they look fake, but I suppose when I get naked with a guy, he'll see the scars. I hadn't really thought of that. At some point when I meet a new guy I suppose I'll just have to be honest. I think a lot of guys quite like fake boobs anyway – it's a Pamela Anderson thing from when they were younger.

The whole idea was to have more confidence and I think I do. Clothes fit *much* better now that I've got something to fill them. I haven't really bought anything new because all my old clothes feel new with a bit of cleavage anyway. I definitely look *better*.

When we went out around Clapham last weekend I did sort of wonder if I'd be fighting men off with a stick, but it was pretty much the same old, just with more guys checking me out, which is fine. I didn't get chatted up any more than normal, really, and Cherise was still the centre of attention. I think I've decided I could have three boobs and she'd still be the centre of attention. I can't lie – the first time we went out and I didn't pull, I was a bit disappointed. I'd built it up to be a big deal in my head . . . and then it was a massive anti-climax.

That said, it's only been a couple of months and I couldn't go out at first anyway. I need to give it more time. I would definitely feel happy getting naked with a guy now if the right one came along. I do think it'll be easier to get a boyfriend now I've had them done.

You know what I think it is? All that build-up – like five years of waiting, and then the worrying about the operation, and then all the soreness and the scars, and all the money, I suppose I thought it was going to be a bigger deal. After all that stress, I expected the world to change, like there should be a parade or something, but it's business as usual. I've been back at work for ages, everyone's pretty much stopped caring that I had it done – even my mum quite likes them now. I thought everything would be more *different*, you know what I mean?

There's no doubt that my boobs look better – I honestly cannot count how many hours I've stared at them for – but they're not *perfect*. I'm a bit pissed off because after all that grief, you would want them to be perfect, right? If you look closely, Ashley is still a tiny bit bigger than Mary-Kate and I reckon the nipple is a little higher too – although I'm clearly a bit obsessed with them.

I don't know, I guess we'll see. I will have to wait a year or two, according to Si, but I might get them done again. Perhaps just a little bit bigger.

I really hope this has been helpful for any of you out there that are thinking about getting your boobs done. Overall I'm really glad I had my surgery. My top tips are: Get a surgeon you really like, find one that's done ops for the NHS (they're better), and make sure you've got someone around to do everything for you right after the op. They are like a million times better, even if I'm not a hundred per cent, and I'm definitely *happier*. I wanted bigger boobs and that's what I got.

Love and hugs

Becca xxx

A Diamond-Encrusted Bubble-Gum-Flavoured Speckled Glittered Brightly Coloured Erotic Eye-Wateringly Bouncy yet Sensible, Comfortable Hammock (with pockets)

LAURA DOCKRILL

Mum, let's pretend we're bakers.
It's 5.30 a.m. and luckily, for us, the cakes have just come out
hot
from the oven.
It's OK; you lie there, because I KNOW you're tired,
And I'll sit here, on your tummy,
with all of my five-year-old body weight
and decorate the cakes. Otherwise referred to as . . .
Your boobs.

Of course I never wanted to *eat* them. I just wanted to
roll
them

and squeeze them.

And attack them.

Because I didn't have *them*.

And when she 'reminded' me that once upon a time, before the plastic joy of McDonald's,

that they *fed* me! I DRANK from them, with my *mouth*?

Well, I was horrified.

And I never wanted to see them again.

They were 'udders'.

Embarrassing ones. With personalities.

I hated seeing friends' mums' ones even more, accidentally; in a changing room,

All baked-egg-like and soggy and depressed and wilting,

Like a flabby rejected exotic plant that nobody read the 'How To Look After' manual of.

When they (the breasts) chased me, and caught me, *got* me, in the kiss chase menace of puberty, I fought, proper.

I said

'NO! Don't give me those' and took to a bra like a fly to a pond. Drowning, terribly.

It meant I was growing up

and I would have to watch whilst my sister

got tickles and ice cream

whilst I awaited Santa's stocking of sanitary towels and M&S vouchers.

Thanks *Papa Chrimbo*.

Cheers for that.
I'm about to explode.
Like a bomb of snake blood.

Then suddenly, they become your *thing* almost overnight.
They are yours.
Flat-chested girls say,
'How did you do that?' about your boobs, and you say
'Just by being alive and eating loads of stuff.'
And that's pretty good and you
look at slightly chubby blokes and think
Thank God I'm not a bloke because they aren't allowed two
sockets for extra fat to dress up in a balcony bra
and you are proud but guilty.
Dockers' Knockers.
Inside I just wanted to be Tinkerbell actually.

We want 'tits' like girls in French films who
shove vest tops on with NOTHING underneath,
who hop and spring around like newly born lambs,
boobies like ice-cream cones,
like hiccups,
like moths,
with nipples like tiny perfect kidney beans.

Those girls want 'bangers' with big moose-like swells,
orbiting their own selves like naked gorilla heads, stuffed into
   swelling stinging frothy elastic,
that punch your lights out every time you go to switch the

light out,
black eyes but . . . look at them boobs.

You go to your friends' houses and you swoon at their
little cup-cake paperette bras dangling on the bathroom door,
like dinky patterned bonnets for Barbie dolls that almost make
you weep, *they are so pretty*.
Meanwhile, should you and your friends ever get stuck on a
desolate cliff?
You could certainly attempt catapulting them across the
world to safety with the capacity of your *BRASSIERE*, that's
right, I dropped the *Brassiere* bomb, code word for flubbery,
gargantuan, goblinesque, dinosauric, vacuous pit of Bermuda
Triangle, no man's land.
It's a *contraption*.
It's a bit of *equipment*. *That's* not pretty.

I also recognise the advantages.
My bra is like a rucksack and can hold loads of stuff inside it.

Because my mum wore low-cut tops and let her boobs harass
    the eyes of strangers
I have always kept mine relatively *under wraps*
like the magazines that come in bags that you're not allowed
a free flick through before purchase.
My chest is a gamble.

I wish you could eat it.
Your bra.

A bra.

Or at least chew from it.

It must have another purpose other than just like Clinton's
   monetising on Valentine's cards,

making men and women curdle sour everywhere,

Well . . . bra shops do the same, with their variety,

they are all too small,

too ugly or just too rubbish,

however,

we need them

because there is NO better feeling in the world than taking a
bra off after a hard day's work of bra wearing. And I've tried
a lot of feelings.

Bra shopping for big boobs is horror of the head syndrome
when every answer is a no.

Because how many hammocks are beautiful? The title of
this piece is actually an advert. That is what I am looking for.

When you finally swan out and the right bits go where they
should,

in and out like the violin they always promised . . .

You feel like a goddess

mixed in with a mistress

mixed in with a fraud

but mostly a bit like a woman.

Which I guess is allowed.

And you are thankful.

That you 'got it' and 'you know it'

But then suddenly,
as if all women are WWE Wrestlers battling it out for the one
golden belt that is their perfect physique, *of course*,
it gets taken (I say taken I mean stolen) away from you the
   moment you found it
and then you yourself wait to be woken up at 5.30 a.m.
and have some other new weird child of your own,
playing bakers with your tits.

JENNY ECLAIR

I used to have a line in my stand-up where I described my breasts as having let me down so much that I now referred to them as 'Brutus and Judus'. The truth is a lot more mundane. They are sturdy and workman-like and mostly fairly reliable. They are not the kind of bosoms that fall out of a bikini top at the sight of a third-division footballer; they are pretty sensible and I kennel them in a Sloggi non-wired 34A cup bra.

If anything my breasts are slightly Nordic. I know this for a fact because the only time I've seen breasts like mine, en masse, was when I went swimming in Finland – all the women there had identical breasts to mine. I like to think there is something of the Viking about them – or maybe I mean troll?

Anyway, as I say, they've never given me much grief, until last year when at the age of fifty-one I was called for my first mammogram. To be honest it wasn't a big deal, we trotted down the road, me and the tits, got them squashed against a screen for scanning and came home.

It was mid-January, I'd finished panto, was doing shifts on the *Loose Women* panel and had just booked a week in Miami. Everything was tickety boob, *Loose Women* had even been nominated for an NTA – a National Television Award, no less! All I had to do was sort out some kind of ensemble/frock for the bash, but I had a week to shop. There was no rush.

Then the letter came. The mammogram result was suspect, and I needed further investigation. They gave me a date to come back and get checked out. It was scheduled for when we were in Miami.

I phoned the hospital to explain, expecting them to say that when I got back from the States would be cool. They didn't – they said I should be seen before I went; in fact I should be seen by the end of the week, Then they said that if further 'exploration' found something more sinister then Miami could possibly be off the agenda as I might require immediate treatment.

Some things make you go cold, they make you go clumsy, they make your head feel like it's underwater and you can't hear properly. I felt sick all the way down to my knees.

I told my partner and I told my daughter and I told my sister. I didn't tell anyone else and I couldn't be bothered to buy a new frock for the NTAs which were being held at the O2 arena the night before I was due to be thoroughly X-rayed. I did however decide that going to the awards would be a welcome distraction and cobbled together a last-minute outfit from the back of my wardrobe. It wasn't great – it involved a silver dress and a vintage coat and some snot-green tights, which I thought gave the outfit a Tilda Swinton twist but just looked a bit mad. I went to the O2 with all the other Loose Women (we didn't win) and at the end of the night when I couldn't find my cab to come home, I may have done some swearing and foot stamping in the car park – but really I was just very frightened of the morning.

My sister came to King's College Hospital with me. She made me walk – I'd have got the bus but she was right, it is only three stops from my house.

An hour later we were walking home – correction, I was skipping. The lump was a collection of tiny water-filled cysts – very common, we were told. Huzzah! Never has south London looked more beautiful, never have my nearest and dearest been more relieved, never have I looked forward to a holiday more . . . Miami we were on our way.

A week or so later, we were at Heathrow. Browsing through the magazines in WHSmith I spotted a headline which screamed, 'Worst Dressed Celebs at the NTAs'! And there I was, lumpy in my vintage coat, non-matching scarf and saggy snot-green tights. All I needed to complete the mad bag woman look was a pram full of cats and some rubbish.

As I looked at that photo and I remembered the worry and the upset and the gut-wrenching fear, I realized I couldn't give a shit about these bitchy magazines with their horrible stupid lists. Me and my tits were off to Miami, and I laughed all the way to the plane.

SOPHIE ELLIS-BEXTOR

Boobs. In the words of the Bloodhound Gang, hooray for boobies.

I have two. They are OK. Not amazing, but not terrible. I have hoisted them in bras, fed three babies with them, wished they were bigger and felt them for lumps, because lumps are the serious side of boobs. My grandma died of breast cancer when I was eleven. I still miss her now.

When I was asked to write about my relationship with my breasts I was a bit perplexed. I love them and yet, it's complicated. Like most girls I have not always reacted in a positive way to my boobs. When I was about ten or eleven the first girls in my class began 'developing', as we called it, and began needing to buy their first bras. I found most of the process mortifying. Cuddling my parents was harder as the new existence of a chest came between us figuratively and literally. I felt I was betraying them by not being a little girl anymore. I then started wearing training bras which my dad – probably pretty mortified himself – called 'bib tops'. This was pretty cringey.

As I entered my teens I began to embrace my new curves a

little more. They weren't going away so I knew I'd better get a handle on them. Aged about thirteen I remember asking my mum if I could go and get a real bra. We finally went to get one and I was a 34D. I felt rather smug about that as she hadn't thought I needed a bra yet. Bib tops were still OK by her. Suddenly – ha! I had a proper bra size and they sounded like they weren't too small, either. This was what I wanted, right? My friends and I then proceeded to spend most of our late teens wearing Wonderbras. It seemed to be that we all wanted a killer cleavage. God, Wonderbras were uncomfy. Fortunately my twenties introduced me to getting properly measured, balconettes, comfort and a happier, less aggressive rack. I haven't looked back except for the times after having my babies when I have endured the joy of nursing bras. Until that point, you don't think there's going to be a time in your life when you will wear whatever it takes to get your boobs out whenever and wherever you are just to feed that baby.

I think all sizes have pros and cons. I have experienced mine big and small. With my pregnancies I've got to try out having really massive boobs. Quite fun and I always miss them a little when they go. That being said, what I have now is fine. A handful but not out of hand.

So what's round the corner? Hopefully we still have some fun times ahead. I will still be hoisting them in bras, possibly feeding another baby with them one day and checking them for lumps. When all is said and done it's the serious side of boobs it comes down to. I hope they stay healthy. I really do miss my grandma.

CAROLINE FLACK

When I was growing up I only had one boob. It was fairly disturbing as I was the only one who knew, and I used to stuff the other side of my bra with tissue. It wasn't until one day when it just got too lopsided that I ran down to the kitchen where my mum was making carbonara and shouted out in despair, 'I'VE ONLY GOT ONE BOOB.' Mum sat me down and told me it was totally normal. Weirdly, within a couple of months I grew a second boob and all was OK. You can rest assured now that I have two fully functioning boobs.

KRISTIN HALLENGA

If boobs could talk they'd demand you to stop being so darn silly. They'd ask you why it is you squeeze them into bras that are quite obviously the wrong size for you and make them feel like they are about to spill over the top and into oblivion. I'm pretty sure they'd also wonder why you or your partner don't give them more attention either; and when they say attention, they mean checking for the signs and symptoms of breast cancer on a regular basis so that you could catch the disease nice and early. They'd tell you to stop being such a ninny because nine out of ten lumps are in fact nothing sinister, but knowing what it is for sure, NOW, is the best defence against the disease that kills so many of your boobs mates every year. Your boobs need you, and until they have a voice (which, quite frankly would be a bit weird, wouldn't it?) I will be telling you and the rest of Britain to check them and give them the love they deserve. Something I stupidly didn't do and now live with breast cancer at twenty-seven because it was detected very late. So, love thy boobies, people!

CHERRY HEALEY

If there were an NSPCC equivalent for boobs then mine would probably be in care. I haven't been very nice to my boobs. In fact, they are suffering from a severe case of neglect.

I've got size 32DD boobies and I do everything in my power to conceal them. I am an expert in minimiser bras (the best ones are from M&S by the way) and finding clothes that hide any hint of a bulge (loose shirts are always a winner). My sports bra is so tight that I struggle to breathe (extremely unhelpful during a legs, bums and tums) and I would feel more comfortable wearing a batman costume than a dress that revealed my cleavage. I don't even like that word. It sounds like an STD. 'I've got a nasty case of cleavage.'

Essentially, what I'd really love are little, pert, cute, size B puppies. You know. Those boobs that don't really need a bra. Those boobs that sit happily up like springer spaniels waiting for treats. Those boobs that laugh in the face of a strapless, silky dress. Ah, how I would love to buy those pretty, lace balcony bras rather than heading straight for the Mammary Gland lingerie.

You see what I mean about being mean? I don't think I've ever said a nice word to my poor glands. They just sit there, doing their job and doing it very well and all I do is complain. Enough.

I've grown up in the Kate Moss era where gamine is God. As a teenager I used to stare at the models in magazines and long for their fragile, boyish frames. It was a time before street style (a wonderful, celebration of different bodies) and TOWIE – big boobs just weren't 'in'.

But I have recently felt a shift in myself. In a world where people pay thousands for painful surgery to enlarge their breasts, I should be embracing my boobies. I should wiggle them and jiggle them and set them free. I should wine them and dine them and dress them up.

The more I realise how ungrateful I've been, the more I realise how ridiculous it is to fight against the body shape you naturally have. Oh the time I've wasted thinking that the grass is greener makes me cringe. After thirty-two years of boob embarrassment, it's now time to give them some love. I need to invest in a few good, pretty bras and maybe even experiment with a bit of cleavage (there's a cream for that I'm sure). I need to remind myself that I Am A Woman and it's OK to have curves. In fact, it's more than OK – it's lovely. And I need to start saying positive things to my breasts. And I must remember not to do this out loud.

Yes, 2013 is the year for Boobie Love, and I'm sure my puppies will appreciate this.

Ben Harris and the Orbs of Power

WILL HILL

Good Friday, 1995

Ben swallowed hard, trying not to let her see the fear in his eyes. He was close.

So close.

It had taken him many months, but he was finally face to face with the culmination of his long, dangerous quest. Now, all that stood between him and triumph were two black semi-circles of cotton and polyester, and a fiendish pair of metal hooks. As he studied this final obstacle, he felt his nerve threatening to betray him, and fought against it.

He had come so far. He would not fail now.

The quest was simple in concept, but no less daunting for its simplicity.

Sean Redman, Ben's best friend and companion on what would undoubtedly be an adventure full of peril and hardship, had summed it up with his usual class and elegance during the last days of the summer holiday, after they had finished watching *Raiders of the Lost Ark* for the hundredth time. He had taken a sheet of A3 paper, written THE ORBS OF POWER at the top in a mediocre approximation of the iconic Indiana Jones lettering, and addressed his friend.

'Tits. Real ones. Female too, no trying to be clever. In the flesh, before the end of the school year.'

Ben had considered this. 'Do we need to touch them, or just see them?'

'The two things sort of go hand in hand, mate,' replied Sean, grinning lasciviously. 'But for the sake of clarity, yeah, you need to touch them. Otherwise walking in on your sister in the shower would qualify. Although in the case of *your* sister, that would be pretty much the best possible result for me.'

'Piss off,' said Ben, mildly. He wasn't really annoyed; Sean had been describing the array of things he would like to do to Chloe in remarkably graphic detail since the first time he had joined Ben's family for dinner after school. It was now just part of their routine.

'Has to be consensual too,' continued Sean. 'No grab and run. Otherwise I'd already be sorted.'

Ben nodded. Sean was an impulsive, risk-taking quester, and had technically already made momentary contact with one of the Orbs of Power, thanks to a remarkably ill-advised single finger prod to the chest of Laura Kelly, who sat behind him in Maths. His foolhardiness had drawn first a gasp of shock, then a furious, bellowed lecture on the subject of personal boundaries, punctuated with a series of vicious blows to his arms and face, delivered with unerring precision by the sharp edge of Laura's Take That ruler.

'One more thing,' said Sean. 'The main thing, actually.'

'What?' asked Ben.

'This is a quest. We take it seriously, or we don't even bother starting. So that means you don't tell anybody, and especially not any girls. They won't understand. All right?'

'Agreed,' said Ben, although he was no longer really listening. His mind, as it often did, had wandered back to when the idea for the adventure had first occurred to him, a moment that was now seared forever into his memory.

He was lying on a sun lounger on a Kefalonian beach ten days earlier, his dad snoring steadily on one side of him, his mum with her nose buried in a bright pink paperback on the other. His sister had gone into town with the friends she had made in their apartment complex, and Ben was considering heading into the sea to cool down. The sun was beating down from the empty blue sky, and he could feel his skin beginning to burn, a tingling sensation that wasn't wholly unpleasant. He sat up, wincing as his back separated slowly from the white plastic of the lounger, and was about to slide his feet into his flip-flops when he saw her.

Saw them.

Her name was Ria, and she was a waitress in the restaurant they had eaten in the previous night, a narrow glass room wedged between the edge of the beach and main drag that was pleasantly amiable for such an obvious tourist trap. It sold Greek salad, prawns that were five times as big as the ones his mum brought home from Tesco on Saturday morning, and fillets of fish so exotic that he was only aware of them from photos in his encyclopaedia: swordfish, mahi-mahi, barracuda, stingray. All of which were available with chips, so as not to completely terrify the majority of the restaurant's clientele.

She had appeared beside their table, a vision of tanned skin, gleaming white teeth and long black hair, and introduced herself. Ben noticed a tiny frown appear on his mother's forehead and a look of outright dislike rise onto Chloe's face, but then Ria leant forward to pass out menus, and he would not have noticed if his mother and sister had got up on the table and started dancing the can-can. The top three buttons of Ria's white shirt were open, revealing a deep, gently curving cleavage that instantly turned his mouth as dry as the Sahara, and a sliver of pale yellow material that whispered of hidden treasure.

She took their order and glided away through the busy restaurant, leaving chaos in her wake. Ben stared blankly at the table, unable to remember what he'd selected from the menu less than thirty seconds earlier, as his dad smoothed down his hair and straightened the collar of his shirt, drawing a wide-eyed look of fury from his wife and an exaggerated roll of the eyes from his daughter. The atmosphere at the table was charged, almost electric, as they waited for their starters. When the food arrived in the unsteady grip of a middle-aged man with a bald head and a face that was running with sweat, half of the family tried their very best to hide their disappointment.

Now she was before him again, silhouetted against the blinding blue sky and gleaming white sand of the beach. She was wearing bikini bottoms that were the same pale yellow he had glimpsed so fleetingly the previous evening, huge round sunglasses, and a pair of white flip-flops.

And that was all.

Ben's breath froze in his lungs as his gaze came to rest on the upper half of her tanned, narrow body. He knew it was wrong to stare, not just at girls but at anyone, had been told so by both his mum and dad on many occasions, but he was simply powerless to resist. Ria was like something from another planet, a world of irreverent beauty and hopeless glamour so completely different to the one he inhabited; she seemed impossible. Her breasts rode high on her chest, full curves of flawless skin that defied gravity and logic. Then his vision was merely full of the beautiful contours of her shoulders and back as she strolled away down the beach.

Beside him, his dad let out a spluttering snore, then rolled over to one side and farted loudly, breaking the spell. His mother tutted with disapproval, before turning her attention back to her novel, unaware that beside her, her son's doors of perception had been thrown open to reveal a bigger, wider, and far more exciting world.

Ben had told Sean about Ria as soon as he got home, his eyes wide and shining as he attempted to convey the power of what he had seen, the essential *glory* of it. His best friend, who liked to consider himself an expert in all things female despite abundant evidence to the contrary, had listened carefully, then asked whether or not he had slipped her one. Ben, who understood the essential concept of 'slipping one' to a girl, but was far from certain on the details, had said no, leading Sean to shake his head solemnly and call him a tosser.

'I would have,' he continued. 'No doubt about it. I slipped one to this barmaid in Benidorm last year. Nineteen she was. Gave her it right in the sand dunes.'

'At night?' Ben asked.

'Course,' laughed Sean. 'Can't be slipping it to girls in front of everyone. You get locked up for that, even in Spain.'

'Don't you have to be home by nine though?'

'Not on holiday, mate. Different rules abroad.'

'And didn't you come back complaining that your mum and dad made you have dinner with them every night?'

'Ah, well,' said Sean, and tipped a wink in Ben's direction. 'That's what I had to say. Couldn't have word getting back to them that I was sneaking out every night after they were asleep.'

'So what are we doing this quest for then? If you slipped it to half of Spain last summer?'

'Kept their clothes on, didn't they?' said Sean, as though it should have been the most obvious thing in the world. 'Sand gets everywhere, mate. You'll find out one day.'

'Right,' said Ben, wondering, not for the first time, exactly how full of shit his best friend really was.

'Are you all right?' asked Grace Matthews, frowning at him. 'You've gone a bit pale.'

Panic held Ben tightly in its grip; his heart felt like it was going to explode, his blood roaring through his head with a sound like crashing waves.

'I'm fine,' he managed. 'Bit too much to drink, that's all.'

Grace cocked her head to one side and frowned. 'How much have you had?'

Ben did frantic maths in his head. 'Not sure,' he said, aiming for nonchalant but missing badly. 'Six or seven cans?'

Grace narrowed her eyes, then burst out laughing. Ben felt as though he had been punched in the soul.

'What's so funny?' he asked.

'*Six or seven*,' she mimicked. '*Just the six. Or maybe seven.*'

'Could have been four,' he allowed, trying to defuse the situation, trying to bring her terrible, ball-shrivelling laughter to an end, but this merely set her off again.

Ben looked at her, at the deep pink that was now filling her cheeks, her wide mouth and her straight white teeth, her eyes squeezed shut, and wondered if there was any scientific basis to the notion of a heart breaking.

'Please stop laughing at me,' he said, his voice little more than a whisper.

Grace did so, and opened her eyes. Ben saw no malice in them, saw nothing but gentleness and kindness, and felt his stomach lurch.

'Sorry,' she said. 'That was mean. But honestly Ben, six or seven cans? There's maybe about eight stone of you, if you're soaking wet. Six or seven cans and I'd be phoning you an ambulance.' She grinned at him, and Ben managed a small smile in return. 'You don't have to make stuff up, trying to impress me,' she continued. 'Bonnie was right. I do like you.'

Ben swallowed hard. 'You do?'

Grace smiled. 'I'm sat on this bed with you with no top on waiting for you to pluck up the courage to touch me. What do you reckon?'

'You can see a nipple on this bit.'

Ben crouched down and scuttled across the garden to where Sean was kneeling in the midst of an overgrown hedge, holding out a scrap of paper triumphantly. Ben grabbed it, and saw that his friend was right; at the edge of the torn rectangle of formerly glossy paper, there rose the unmistakable shape of a nipple, the skin dark pink and uneven.

'Wicked,' said Ben. 'Any more?'

'Most of the mag's in here,' replied Sean, turning back into the hedge and reaching through its branches. They raked at his skin, leaving the faint red lines that Sean called chicken scratches on his arms and hands, but he didn't appear to notice; his mind was completely focused on digging for treasure.

The quest for the Orbs of Power had been underway for more than a month, although frustratingly little real progress had been made. Sean had immediately attempted to secure glory for himself by making a move on what he referred to as his 'sure thing', a girl from the other half of the year named Amy who had carried a passionate, somewhat inexplicable, torch for him throughout most of Year Ten.

Unfortunately for Sean, she had eventually grown tired of waiting for him to acknowledge her existence and was now seeing a boy from the other half of the year who Ben played football with and who, Amy had told Sean with obvious pride and no small amount of relish, was apparently 'hung like one of them horses'. Sean had taken this revelation with his usual level of dignity, and had eventually been forced to apologise for some of his less polite comments after Amy had pointed out that her new boyfriend's older brother had just got out of prison, and had what his family referred to as 'a bit of a temper'.

'Check this out,' said Sean, and passed him a second muddy page from the depths of the hedge. Ben looked at it and frowned; the image was such a close-up that he didn't have the slightest idea what he was looking at. There was pink skin, and red folds, and something that might have been blonde hair at the very edge of the page.

'Brilliant,' he said, without enthusiasm.

Sean loved nothing more than rooting through disused gardens and car parks, searching out discarded pages of the top-shelf magazines that often caught Ben's eye in the newsagent. They were a surprisingly common find, and Sean saw them as a treasure trail that should be diligently followed, benevolently left by older and wiser men for the education of the teenagers that found them. Ben, on the other hand, couldn't help wondering why they had been discarded in the first place. Presumably either the previous owner had been trying to get rid of them, or was finished with them; both options that filled him with the sudden desire to take a shower.

He had been reduced to scavenging for discarded porn by what he would forever think of as The *Playboy* Incident. Kev Simmons, the goalkeeper for Ben's Saturday morning football team, worked a paper round for the newsagent's on the high street, and was the closest thing they had to a Morgan Freeman in *The Shawshank Redemption*; someone who can get things for you. Mr Grey, who owned the newsagent's, was known to occasionally look the other way when it came to age-restricted items, provided he was asked about them when the shop was empty. As a result, Kev had been able to acquire a couple of packets of B&H, a four-pack of McEwan's lager, and eventually, after several requests (in Mr Grey's hierarchy looking at naked women was clearly potentially more damaging than drinking alcohol or inhaling poisonous smoke), the crown jewel: a slightly water-damaged copy of *Playboy*.

Everything about it was exotic; the square shape, the adverts for unfamiliar brands and products, the prices listed in dollars and cents. And, of course, page after page of naked girls, the vast majority of them tanned, blonde beneficiaries of the finest enhancements that the American plastic surgery industry had to offer. Their breasts stood out high and round like footballs, their skin glowed with airbrushed perfection, their legs seemed to go on forever, and their friendly, cheerful smiles were full of straight white teeth.

After several rounds of pleading, the final one sweetened by a promise to pass on to Kev one of the pictures of his sister in a bikini that had been taken in Kefalonia, an agreement had finally been made to lend the magazine to Ben for one week. The exchange had been made after football practice one Wednesday evening, the magazine making its way from Kev's bag to Ben's at such speed that any casual observer would likely not have realised that the transfer had taken place. Ben had rushed home, showered the football mud off himself, then locked the bathroom door and settled down to examine his prize. He had just unfolded the glorious, jaw-dropping centrefold and placed it on the bathroom floor so that he could better take in its full majesty, when his dad had shoved open the bathroom door, sending the treacherous lock tumbling to the floor. He had taken a step into the room, caught sight of his son sat on the toilet with his jeans around his ankles and a two-foot long photo of a naked blonde woman called Neriah looking up at the ceiling, and frozen. For an interminably long moment, neither of them had moved. Then finally Ben's dad's paralysis had broken; he had shouted 'Jesus Christ' before disappearing so quickly it was as though he had been yanked out of the bathroom by a bungee cord.

The subsequent conversation, after Ben had gathered himself together and made his way downstairs on legs that felt like jelly, had been excruciating, not least because his dad had chosen to open it with, 'Look, son, men like looking at tits. It doesn't matter how old they are. I still like looking at them and I'm three times your age.' His follow-up line, in which he informed his son that every woman in the world had them, including his mother and his sister, had sounded to Ben like some terrible threat, rather than the casual demystification that was intended, and the exchange had rapidly devolved into a seemingly infinite purgatory of burning red faces and mortified stuttering.

The *Playboy* Incident had been the devastating end of a long-running series of attempts to familiarise himself more thoroughly with the subject of the quest that he and Sean had embarked upon: the Orbs of Power themselves.

He had stared in open-mouthed awe at naked women in softcore thrillers on cable movie channels late at night, sitting inches away from his small television in the dark, his ears plugged with headphones: tanned, bottle-blonde Americans with perfectly spherical breasts who bounced enthusiastically on top of men with side-parted hair, throwing their hair from side to side, screeching like banshees.

He had accompanied Sean to his friend's cousin's house one lunchtime, where the three of them had silently watched the porn video that Sean's cousin kept inside a box labelled *Match of the Day*, which was perhaps twenty years old, and at least a fifteenth- or sixteenth-generation copy. It contained the first penis Ben had ever seen apart from his own, and there were unquestionably real people actually having real sex in front of the camera, but it was a monotonous blur, and he found himself increasingly focusing on the sets and the costumes; the lead actress was dressed, when she was wearing clothes, as Cleopatra, a character in one of the plays they were studying in English.

He had also investigated the supposed orgy of imagery that was becoming available on something new called the internet. A couple of kids from school had it, and one of them, Matthew Hetherington, had held forth on the subject at great length during form a week or two earlier.

'Mate, you can see whatever you want. It's incredible.'

'How come?' Ben had asked.

'You just search for stuff. There's this thing, it's called AltaVista. You type in, like, porn or whatever. Or big tits. Then you press SEARCH and it finds pictures of them for you.'

Ben frowned. 'Where from?'

'What?'

'Where does it find them from?'

'How am I supposed to know that? It just does. You need to tell your mum to get it, mate, seriously.'

Ben had duly asked his mother about the possibility of their getting the internet, but had been unable to provide an answer when she asked him why he wanted it. He was sure that 'So I can look at porn without having to creep around in disused gardens' would not be what his mother wanted to hear. So instead, he had made an effort to befriend Matthew Hetherington, in the hope of getting access to the portal of sexual delight that apparently sat innocuously on his dad's desk in the upstairs office. But after several interminable lunch breaks spent listening to the intricacies of rugby union, a sport that left Ben scratching his head in confusion but seemed to be the central axis of Matthew's life around which everything else revolved, he had given up on the idea. Nothing was worth another lecture on the correct strategy to deploy when defending a line-out.

Not even the Orbs of Power.

'This is bollocks, mate,' said Ben, throwing aside the scrap of soiled porn. 'We're getting nowhere.'

'What are you on about?' asked Sean, from within the hedge.

'This,' said Ben. 'The quest. All of it. Nothing's happening, mate. Just because we decided to be on a quest and you wrote it down in Indiana Jones lettering doesn't mean anything's changed.'

'Stop whining, for Christ's sake,' said Sean. 'You didn't have a girl threatening to have some prison nutcase cut your balls off unless you apologised to them. Could be worse.'

'There you go though,' said Ben. 'Tom Richards is the same year as us and he looks like he's been smashed in the face with a hammer. But he's having it away with Amy Dillon now, and she used to fancy *you*. Kev Simmons told me Olivia Bell let him put his hand up her skirt last week after Drama Club. Kev. Simmons. Yet neither of us can manage to touch a girl's tits. I mean, seriously, what the hell is wrong with us? Is that so much to ask from the universe?'

'Never mind the universe. Have you asked any girls?'

'Asked them to let me touch their tits?'

'Yeah.'

'Of course not,' said Ben. 'I saw what happened to you with Laura Kelly.'

'That's different though,' said Sean. 'I never asked her, did I? That's why she got all uptight about it.'

Right, thought Ben. *I'm sure that's why.*

'So what are you suggesting?' he asked.

'Jesus mate, I don't know,' said Sean, ceasing his digging and turning to face his friend. 'Do I have to think of everything? What about that girl in the year above?'

'What girl in the year above?'

'You know. Grace something.'

Ben froze. 'Grace Matthews?'

'That's her. You haven't done anything about that, have you? So you can't be that arsed.'

'About. What?'

Sean frowned. 'Did I not tell you she likes you?'

'Were you supposed to tell me she likes me?'

'Yeah. Her mate Bonnie whatserface told me to tell you.'

'So why didn't you?'

'Christ, I don't know. I've been a bit busy, mate, with this quest we're both supposed to be on.'

'You're a complete twat. Do you know that?'

Sean's frown deepened. 'What's the big deal, mate? Did you fancy her or something? I've never heard you mention her.'

Ben considered this. He had never really thought about Grace Matthews in those terms, or any of the Year Eleven girls for that matter. They were invariably seen in the company of boys from the Sixth Form College, boys with cars and motorbikes and unconvincing facial stubble who could successfully get served in pubs.

'No,' he said. 'But that's not the point. You should have told me, mate. We're supposed to be in this together.'

'Jesus, don't cry about it. Bonnie only told me last week. I'm sure Grace is still interested.'

'You're sure?'

'Well, no. I mean, to be honest, she's probably thinks you bottled sending her a message back. But there could still be a chance. Like, a really small one. So that's something, eh?'

The next morning Ben walked to school with his heart pounding against his ribs, his palms clammy, and his legs feeling like they were made of jelly. His plan was simple; get through maths and English, track down Bonnie Dean during first break, send a message via her to Grace Matthews, meet up with Grace at lunchtime, and be well on the way to completing his quest by the end of school.

The first part of the plan went perfectly. Ben safely negotiated an hour of sines and cosines, along with one of Mr Barrington's characteristic tangents into how best to survive a nuclear apocalypse, including a basic rations list and the best places to buy a home Geiger counter. English too appeared to be passing without incident, as Ben answered a couple of early questions regarding the setting and atmosphere of Charles Dickens' *Hard Times* and then settled down for what should have been forty minutes of blissful, relaxing obscurity.

Then, with barely five minutes to go until the bell would have rung for morning break, Mrs James caught him doodling breasts of all shapes and sizes in the margins of his exercise book. This in itself was not disastrous, worthy of no more than a sharp telling-off after the bell, and the loss of a minute or two of his break time. Unfortunately for Ben, his mind was already rehearsing what he was going to say to Bonnie Dean when he tracked her down, and he responded to his English teacher with two words that would haunt his nightmares for months to come.

'Sorry, Mum.'

There was a moment of incredulous silence, then the rest of the class burst into laughter of a volume and ferocity that Ben had never before encountered. At that moment, the trail that led towards the Orbs of Power, the trail which had seemed on the verge of bursting thrillingly, brilliantly into life in the Year Eleven shape of Grace Matthews, disappeared along with his social life and, or so it seemed to Ben, any possibility of his life ever again being anything other than cold and miserable.

'So how come you never asked me out?'

Ben considered this, trying to keep this attention on Grace's pale, lovely face and not on the black bra that was hovering at the lower edge of his vision, taunting him. 'I was going to,' he said, eventually. 'But Sean didn't give me your message for about a week and he didn't think you would still be interested, and then the thing in Mrs James' class happened, and after that I was sure you wouldn't be.'

'Your mate Sean's a moron. You know that, right?'

Ben frowned. 'He's all right.'

'No,' said Grace. 'He's not. He's a moron.'

'I know,' said Ben, loyalty twisting in his gut. 'I mean, I get why you would think so. But when you get to know him . . .'

'I would never want to,' said Grace. 'And you'd be better off without him. I think you know it, too.'

'Maybe,' allowed Ben. 'But then, I've known him since I was six.'

'I've known the kid next door to me who eats his own snot since I was three. Doesn't mean I have to be friends with him.'

Ben grinned. 'Fair enough.'

'None of my business, like. Do whatever you want. But I reckon you'll see I'm right, eventually.'

Ben struck out for safer ground. 'Who's your best mate? Bonnie?'

Grace appeared to consider this. 'I suppose so.'

'You aren't sure?'

'Not really. I mean, I am sure that she's my best friend now. But I'm not going to spend the rest of my life in this crappy little town, so I like to think that I haven't met whoever my real best friend is going to be yet.'

'What if you don't meet anyone you like more than Bonnie?'

Grace laughed. 'That would be very disappointing. But maybe I won't. Maybe I'll be a friendless loser for the rest of my life. Or maybe I'll meet the coolest people in the world

66

and go on adventures with them. Who knows? That's what makes it all so exciting.'

'What?'

'Life, silly.'

Ben blushed. 'Right,' he muttered. 'Of course. Sorry.'

There was silence in the bedroom, a long moment of it that wasn't remotely uncomfortable; to Ben it felt warm and fuzzy, like he was surrounded by invisible cotton wool. He was trying to focus on his quest, on the goal that, as he stole a glance at the raised pattern on the edges of the black bra, he realised was literally within his reach, but Grace Matthews kept distracting him, kept disarming him with her easy confidence, her way of making things seem clear and simple, her straightforward honesty and her obvious disinterest in games or bullshit.

'Ben,' she said, after an unknown amount of time had passed.

'What?'

'Look at me, Ben.'

He raised his gaze from where he had been studying the pattern of stripes and squares on the duvet cover. Grace was sat with her legs crossed and her elbows resting on her knees, her body leant slightly towards him, an unreadable expression on her face.

'Why are you so nervous?' she asked.

Ben suddenly realised two things. Firstly, that he was about to break the solemn promise he had made to Sean. Secondly, that there was a good chance he was about to say one of the stupidest things that a teenage boy had ever said to a partially undressed teenage girl. He drew a deep breath, and took the plunge.

'I'm on a quest.'

The winter months were cold, and hard.

Children have long memories, teenagers especially, and Ben's hope that referring to Mrs James as 'Mum' would soon be forgotten proved hopelessly naïve. The outright insults and mocking died down, as new embarrassments presented themselves, but the incident remained lurking just below the surface, ready to be brought back up whenever he did anything even remotely worthy of derision. Even Sean had taken to keeping his distance, not wanting to be tainted with his best friend's sudden, catastrophic fall from grace, and appeared to have lost all interest in their quest. He was now spending most evenings at Matthew Hetherington's house playing something called *DOOM* and showing worrying signs of a burgeoning interest in rugby.

Ben kept his head down, let his contribution to the success of the school football team prevent his stock from ever bottoming out completely, and devoted himself to the quest for the Orbs of Power, which was now approaching the status of an obsession. He blamed the quest for what had happened in Mrs James's class, had started, in all honesty, to believe that the trajectory of his life had somehow become bound up with it, that things would not improve until he completed it.

Cursed, he thought to himself one evening, as his father snored through *Match of the Day* and his mother chatted happily away on the phone to her sister. *It's like the quest has put a curse on me.*

* * *

As is so often the case where quests are concerned, it was when things seemed at their bleakest, when the path seemed blocked at every turn, that a chink of light shone through the clouds, illuminating a possible way ahead.

Sean's parents had gone to their timeshare villa in Florida for two weeks, as they had been doing every Easter holiday for as long as anyone could remember, and his sister Cheryl, who was home from university, had announced that she was going to Edinburgh with her friends on Good Friday and would not be back until the afternoon of Easter Sunday. Which could only mean one thing.

House party.

Sean had persuaded Kev Simmons to push out all the stops, and had managed to acquire four crates of cheap French lager. Matthew Hetherington was going to DJ, having allegedly learnt how to do so in Ibiza the previous summer, and pretty much the entire year was invited, even Ben. He was more relieved than he would ever have admitted to anyone; he had been deeply unsure whether he would make the cut. And as the day approached, the gloom that had settled over him during the winter months was lifted even further by a message, this time delivered to him personally by Bonnie Dean, that Grace Matthews was looking forward to seeing him at the party. Why this would be so was unclear to him, such had been his recent status as a social pariah, but he didn't question it; he merely added it to the ever-growing pile of evidence that reinforced his conviction that girls were simply impossible to understand.

When Good Friday finally arrived, Ben paired his best YSL shirt with black jeans and Reebok classics, applied a liberal amount of gel to his hair, and headed off to what he hoped would be a date with destiny, the completion of a quest that had threatened to take over his life, to drag him ever further downwards.

This is it, he thought, as he walked the short distance to Sean's house. *This is the night everything changes.*

Two hours later, he was standing exactly where he always ended up at parties: with Sean and Kev in the kitchen, sipping lager he wasn't enjoying and screaming silently at himself to go and talk to someone, to talk to a girl, any girl.

You play for the football team. You get good marks. You're not that bad looking. Stop being so completely PATHETIC.

'This party,' announced Kev, 'is really, really shit.'

'Piss off,' said Sean. 'It's not got going yet, that's all.'

'Oh, it's going,' said Kev, gesturing out towards the living room, which was full of boys and girls from their year and the one above dancing and laughing as Matthew poured tune after tune out of a pair of turntables he had brought with him. This had been greeted with open astonishment by his friends, who had assumed Matthew had been lying about being able to mix. 'We're just not on board.'

Sean had no response, as what Kev was saying was demonstrably, painfully true. Instead, he opened another can of lager and took a long swig, trying not to grimace at the taste. Ben watched him, already weighing up which line he was going to use when he told his friends he was leaving; the party was already on the verge of becoming unbearable, and he had no appetite for masochism. Then Kev elbowed him hard in the ribs.

'What the hell?' he asked, glaring at his friend, who merely widened his eyes, as though he was trying to alert Ben to something.

A light cough sounded from behind him, and Ben turned towards the source of it. Grace Matthews was standing in the doorway of the kitchen, holding a bottle of wine in her hand and smiling at him.

'So,' she said. 'This is where all the cool people are.'

Sean and Kev erupted in fake laughter, but Ben didn't join in; he was looking at Grace. Her blonde hair was tied back in a loose ponytail and she was wearing a blue top with white edging and a denim skirt that stopped halfway up her long, pale thighs. Her breasts were gentle swells beneath the blue material of her top, but it hadn't even occurred to him to look at them; he was wondering why he had never noticed how pretty she was, how stop-the-clocks, pause-the-CD beautiful.

Focus! screamed the part of his brain in which the quest, and everything it had come to mean, resided. *This is your chance! You can be done with this tonight! You can finally be free!*

But Ben couldn't focus; he stared at Grace Matthews without a thought in his head, and when she skipped lightly across the kitchen, took his hand and announced to Sean and Kev that she was stealing their friend for a while, he let himself be stolen without a single word of protest.

Grace led him up the stairs and into Sean's sister's room. One of Ben's hands was enveloped inside one of hers, the other clutching desperately onto the can of lager he had been drinking before she appeared; at that precise moment, as she

71

pushed him into the bedroom and closed the door, it seemed to be the only thing that made any sense to him.

'So,' she said, turning to face him. 'Hi.'

Ben burst out laughing. 'Hi,' he said. 'You all right?'

'I am,' she replied, setting the wine bottle on the bedside table and hopping gracefully up onto the bed. 'I'm having a perfectly lovely time. You?'

'I am now,' he said.

Smooth, whispered his quest-brain. *That's the stuff. More of that.*

'Are you just going to stand there?' asked Grace.

'Course not,' said Ben, and settled onto the bed with as much elegance as he was able, keeping a respectful distance between them.

'Cool,' she replied. 'So. Ben. Why exactly did you call Mrs James your mum?'

A black hole of shame opened up inside Ben's stomach, and his skin began to tingle with embarrassed heat. 'What?' he managed.

'Come on,' said Grace. 'Like we were going to be able to get away with not mentioning it? It's not that big a deal, Ben, really it isn't. I don't know why you let everyone give you so much shit about it.'

'I didn't *let* them,' said Ben. 'I couldn't stop them.'

'You let it bother you, though. That's what feeds them. That's what kept it going.'

'I know,' said Ben. 'But . . . I called a teacher Mum. Seriously. Out loud. There didn't seem to be any way I could get out of it.'

'You did, didn't you?' said Grace, and started to giggle. 'You called your English teacher Mum.'

Ben felt himself start to smirk. 'Yeah,' he said. 'Right in front of everyone.'

Grace burst out laughing, and he felt himself surrender to the infectious sound, felt himself begin to laugh about something that he had believed had come to define him but now felt utterly insignificant. He howled with laughter, rolling onto his side and clutching at his ribs, feeling months of misery and self-hatred spill out of his open mouth. Grace had buried her face in a pillow and seemed to be having trouble breathing, she was laughing so hard; Ben hoped she was all right, as there was absolutely nothing he could do to help her if she wasn't.

Eventually, the tidal wave of laughter began to subside. He gasped for air, as Grace slowly lifted her head and looked at him.

'Bonnie talked to you,' she said. 'Right?'

Ben nodded.

'What did she she tell you?'

Ben swallowed hard. 'She told me that you were looking forward to seeing me at the party . . .'

'And?'

' . . . and that she thought you might still like me. Although I don't think I was supposed to tell you she said that.'

Grace smiled. 'It's all right. I won't tell her off too badly.'

Ben was suddenly very aware of the temperature in the bedroom; it was as though someone was steadily turning up the thermostat, sucking all the moisture out of him. He was incredibly aware of his tongue, and his mouth felt as dry and rough as sandpaper. 'Okay,' he said.

Grace tilted her head to one side. '*Are* you okay?' she asked. 'You've gone a bit red.'

'I'm fine,' he said.

'Are you nervous around me?'

'Course not.'

'Because you don't have to be.'

'I'm not nervous.'

'You are. I can tell. Maybe this will relax you. Or maybe not.'

Grace reached down and with an effortless raising of her arms, brought the blue top over her head and threw it onto the floor. She smiled as he stared at her, the colour draining from his face, his mind empty apart from the screeching, triumphant voice of his quest-brain.

This is it! This is going to happen! It's happening! DON'T SCREW IT UP!

'A quest? What are you talking about?'

Ben could feel his cheeks beginning to burn. He didn't know why he had suddenly decided to bare his soul to Grace Matthews, but he was committed now; there was no going back.

'Like a pact,' he said. 'Me and Sean Redman.'

Grace rolled her eyes. 'Christ. This isn't going to be good, is it?'

'I don't know,' said Ben. 'It seemed like fun when we started it, but now I'm not sure. I think it might be sort of stupid.'

Grace leant back against the pile of pillows at the end of the bed and folded her arms across herself. Ben tried not to notice how her forearms pushed her breasts up and in, creating a cleavage that threatened to render him incapable of conscious thought. 'Come on then,' she said. 'Out with it.'

'It was after I came back from Kefalonia last summer,' said Ben. 'There was this waitress . . .'

'There was, was there?' asked Grace. 'Did you have a little holiday romance with her?'

Ben shook his head. 'No. I never spoke to her. But I saw her . . . on the beach . . .'

'In a bikini?' asked Grace. There was a set to her jaw, a certain straightness to her mouth that made Ben suspect she was already several steps ahead of him.

'No.'

'*Not* in a bikini?'

'Yeah. Well, sort of. Top half.'

'So you saw some Greek girl topless on the beach. What's the big deal?'

Ben said nothing. He couldn't work out how to articulate why the moment had seemed so important to him, why it had sent him home lit from within by some unknown fire, ready to make pacts and start quests. After a long moment, Grace spared him.

'Oh for Christ's sake,' she said, rolling her eyes and fixing him with a look of intense disappointment. 'They were probably the first tits you'd ever seen apart from your mum's, weren't they?'

Ben didn't reply.

'Jesus, why are all boys so stupidly *predictable*?' she asked, her pale cheeks starting flush pink. 'What the hell is it with all of you and tits? You're like dogs after a bone. Tell me this quest then, you might as well. What was it, who could be the first to get a girl to show you hers?'

'Sort of,' managed Ben. 'We had to . . . touch . . .' His voice faded away to nothing, driven back into his throat by the look on Grace Matthews' face.

'You're on a quest to see who can be the first to touch a girl's tits? Is that what you're telling me?'

'I . . .'

'Because you know how pathetic that sounds, right?'

'I do. But I . . . didn't. Until now.'

'And you heard that I liked you, so you thought I was your best shot?'

Ben stared helplessly at her.

'Do you know why I liked you?' asked Grace, her eyes blazing. 'Because I thought you might be different. I can get this sort of crap from any of the boys in our year, could go downstairs right now and get it from any of the dickheads dancing around in the living room. You, though? You're sort of awkward, and you try to hide how clever you are, which pisses me off, but you've always been nice to me and I thought you might be a good person, that you might have something about you, something more going on that just football and cider and trying to shove your hand up girls' skirts. So maybe your mate Sean *is* the smart one, because I'm clearly the idiot here.'

Ben reached out a hand towards her, trying to somehow bridge the gap that had yawned open between them. Grace slapped it away, then sat forward, reached behind her back and unhooked the black bra. It fell into her lap as she sat up straight and fixed her eyes on his.

'Come on then,' she said. 'Let's get this over with.'

Ben's eyes widened. 'What are you –'

'Do what you came up here with me to do. Touch me. Finish your stupid little quest if it means so much to you, then we can

76

go back downstairs and I can try and find someone I actually like to talk to.'

She reached out, grabbed his wrists, and pulled his hands forward, guiding them towards her breasts. Ben realised what was happening a millisecond before it was too late, and pulled back. For a moment his hands trembled as they were pulled in opposite directions, until Ben managed to free them from her grip and plant them firmly onto the duvet cover.

'What's the matter?' she asked, her gaze locked with his. 'I thought this was what you wanted?'

'So did I,' he said.

'So what do you want now?'

'I don't know,' said Ben. 'Not this.'

Grace tilted her head to one side, and regarded him with an unreadable expression. 'What about your quest?'

'To hell with it,' he said, and smiled. 'It was stupid. *I'm* stupid. And I'm sorry I involved you in it. I'm really sorry.'

Grace stared at him for a long moment. Eventually, a small smile rose on her face.

'It's all right,' she said. 'I'm going to get dressed now. Look away.'

Ben nodded, and shuffled himself round on the duvet, fixing his eyes on the far wall of Cheryl's bedroom. A full-length mirror stood beside a chest of drawers, reflecting what was happening behind him, and he fought the urge to take a single glance into it, one last action in pursuit of a quest he no longer wanted any part of.

'Okay,' said Grace, and he turned back to look at her. The blue top was back in place and the colour was fading from her cheeks. Her hair was messy where she had pulled the top over her head, long strands of it hanging loosely around her ears and down towards her neck.

'How do I look?' she asked.

'Good,' he replied.

Grace rolled her eyes. 'Good? Is that all? Jesus, there is so much I have to teach you.'

'Okay,' he said. The thought of being taught anything by Grace Matthews suddenly seemed like the best thing in the world. 'I'm a fast learner.'

She laughed. 'I bet you are. Come sit next to me.'

Ben made his way up the bed, and flopped down beside her. He raised his knees so they formed an arch, and felt a shiver of excitement rush through him as she rested hers against him.

'What's your favourite colour?' he asked. His reserves of small talk, never particularly overflowing, were dangerously close to empty.

She frowned momentarily, then smiled. 'Green. What's yours?'

'Blue,' he said. 'Pale blue.'

'Why did you tell me about your quest? You must have known I wasn't going to like it.'

Ben nodded. 'I did. But I didn't want to lie to you.'

Her smile widened, and she inclined her head slightly towards his. 'Yeah? Why not?'

'I don't know. It just seemed important. It seemed like –'

Her lips stopped his words. Ben's eyes widened, then slowly closed, as the world he knew faded to black around him.

RUFUS HOUND & SIMITCHELL

Being asked to contribute to this illustrious tome has been a great honour, but not without its problems.

What should I offer? Research is clearly the key. A quick websearch yielded some truly staggering information that I, for one, was utterly amazed by. So fantastical, indeed, that I felt mere words could not do it justice. What I needed (or, in other words, what I believed you needed) were pictures.

Fortunately, my chum Mr Simon Mitchell is a dab hand with a set of felt-tips, and so, with chests swollen, eyes open and brains delicately poached, we present to you:

WHAT WE FOUND OUT ON THE INTERNET ABOUT

Fans of Boobies should head to the coast, and see them in their natural habitat.

Expert hunters, they plummet into the sea and catch their prey underwater. Air sacs under the skin cushion the impact.

Their name was possibly based on the Spanish slang term *bobo*, meaning 'stupid', as they had a habit of landing aboard ships, where they were easily captured and eaten.

Owing to this, Boobies are often
mentioned as having been caught and
eaten by shipwrecked sailors, notably
Captain William Bligh of the *Bounty*.

There are many different types of
Booby – Abbott's Booby, Blue-footed
Booby, Red-footed Booby and . . .

... THE MASKED
BOOBY!

The Masked Booby prefers deeper waters than other Boobies, feeding on flying fish and occasionally large squid.

Its nest is strictly symbolic, having no structural value and consisting of small stones, pieces of coral, feathers etc. Its eggs are laid in a slight depression on the bare ground.

The Masked Booby has even been observed riding on the backs of sea turtles when far out at sea.

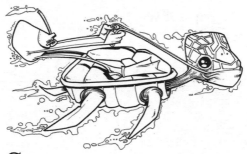

So, the next time danger strikes and *you're* all 'out to sea', maybe you can call upon the incredible aquatic power of

THE MASKED BOOBY!

A Trip Down Mammary Lane

AMY HUBERMAN

Going to the shops with my mum
Was the same old boring humdrum
She never seemed to listen
As I'd see the goods in the shop windows glisten
I yearned for all the stuff I could see
So badly I wanted to pee

Passing another shop door, my tongue would scrape on the floor
'Mum! This window! Look at those puppies!', I'd shout
'You're not ready, not now' and I'd furrow my brow
What was she on about?
Passing the dairy shop entrance
She would sigh with a waited temperance
'Mum, I want them! Those milk jugs!'
And she'd pull me along with her tugs
Next up it was the baps on display
As the baker stood mixing his whey

The cans in the store, the melons galore
The kegs in the pub, the man selling balloons while eating his grub
The funbags on sale midst all of the toys
Being stared at and played with by all of the boys
The scooters with hooters and tonkas with honkers
I wanted them so badly it was driving me bonkers!

And then finally one day
After years of dedicated pray
I gazed in the mirror with a dumbfounded stare
Had someone actually answered my prayer?
Sweet Lord I finally had a pair!
And it was then that I knew what my mum had meant
I'd have been all shopped out with my money spent
When there was no need to panic; the process was much more organic
I jumped in the air and shouted 'Hoorah!'
But then I thought 'Shit', I have to shop for a bra.

JAMEELA JAMIL

My breasts and I, as with any relationship, I suppose, have had our ups and downs. Although I can sufficiently say, since heading past ye olde twenty-five mark, it's more a case of downs. Literally. But we had our glory days once upon a cleavage – long, long . . . LONG ago. I had few attributes growing up; I was far too tall, socially inept, incredibly chubby, spotty, train tracked and worst of all, I considered the lunch ladies to be my only friends at school. But to compensate for the arse I was dealt (an arse that DARED to be both big AND flat!), God (or whoever) bestowed upon me some enormously capacious knockers. They were the light(s) at the end of my dark teenage tunnel. Though I am sad to say that for the first few years of our time shared together, I was deeply ashamed by them. I felt as though they were unwelcome squatters on my chest, I found their size embarrassing and attention-seeking. They completely stole my thunder from age thirteen onwards. Always entering the room SEVERAL seconds before me, constantly introducing themselves to strangers before my face even had a chance, and blocking my view of the television if I ever tried to watch telly lying down in bed, not to mention their knack for turning running for a bus into a game of volleyball. The day I was measured in John Lewis and was forced to buy a 38HH bra, I remember weeping. Hating my father for it, because they are without doubt inherited from him. He's known for his ample bosom. Still quite firm for a man in his sixties. I would spend hours constructing diversion techniques by stooping and swanning around in oversize men's shirts.

Looking back, I feel deeply ashamed of my animosity, and more so . . . naivety. What I saw as impostors were actually loyal friends in disguise. Assets I didn't realise could one day become something of a currency in the bedroom and, the feminist in me is loathe to admit, almost everywhere else. And yet, in what I now look back at as their glory days, I took them totally for granted. Since my teen years, I've lost five stone. A large portion, as with most women, came off my décolletage, and now where those mountains once stood proud, lies a very unimpressive pair of molehills. Molehills that with every year try to run further and further away from my face. I have this recurring nightmare that by my fifties I shall be able to wrap them around my neck and fashion some sort of new age (or old age) bow tie out of them. (She shudders.)

Nonetheless, I'm glad we had some time together. I would like to take this opportunity to formally apologise to my breasts for the years of abuse and neglect I subjected them to, all the sports bras two sizes too small that I shoved and folded them into trying to flatten them down, for all those times I huffed and puffed because I insisted they made everything I wore look slutty (when actually, looking back, I realised, I just bought slutty clothes), for holding them hostage under thick material, never to see the light of day. Breasts, at any size or shape, are a miracle. They are the food with which we nourish our children, they are the collateral with which we negotiate with lovers, and come on, let's face it, whatever they look like, you have to admit we got lucky, we could have had balls . . . imagine that.

The Wall and the Door

MAUREEN JOHNSON

It was a very hot autumn when I first arrived at my Catholic girls' school, aged thirteen, non-Catholic, clueless, never having faced a nun before in my life. Why I was sent there has never been made clear. This is the kind of thing that passes for a joke in my family. And during that very hot autumn, the order lost one sister a week for the first five weeks of school, as if on schedule. Every week, we were taken to the chapel to see them. We knelt and said prayers I did not know directly in front of the bodies of people I had never met in life. I'd only seen a few dead bodies in my life, so five was a lot. That they were all nuns was deeply disorienting. And for a while, it looked like this was how things were always going to be at our school. Someone was going to die every single week. But it wasn't. It was just a bad five weeks, and it earned us the name the Freshmen of Death.

I felt that this was a bad thing, in that distant way that you do when you hear about the death of someone you do not know. You do not want anyone to die. You do not want people to be sad. But when you do not know the deceased, it can be hard to truly engage in what is going on. The five deaths that greeted our arrival almost seemed to fit the strange new surroundings I was in.

There were constant reminders that we were mortal, we were all going to die. There were prayers about it, songs about it, rituals to aid us, statues that depicted it. We said the Hail Mary every morning and before every class, imbedding the words 'now and at the hour of our death' into my brain. I said it in three different languages every day. There was a giant painting by the front door of our school showing nuns of our order bravely standing up to Nazis, and being mowed by machine guns and falling into a mass grave. That was how we greeted you. I had never seen so much death before. It was like I had arrived at Death Prep.

But there was life as well. Potential. We were constantly being told that we were blossoming young women, young and fertile. Too many comparisons were made to flowers. Our bodies were the source of constant commentary. It started before we even got to school, at our mid-summer uniform fitting before freshman year. We were sized not according to our current shape and person, but to the blossoming young woman we would become.

By this, I mean our chest size. See, we wore these tight vests. Well, they were tight in theory. They would be tight when the blossoming had happened. But as pre-freshmen, our petals still closed, it was hard to tell just how much lily there was to gild. And your vest had to last you for four years – you didn't get a new uniform every year. Which is why they employed the Amazing Breast-Size Guessing Nun.

The A.B.S.G.N. would take one look at us, spin us around, and then proclaim our fate in the form of our vest size. She would proclaim it VERY, VERY LOUDLY. ACROSS THE GYM. Because, of course, the sister taking down the sizes was sitting all the way across the room. Why? Why not! It made it more fun for everyone.

'SMALL!' the A.B.S.G.N. would yell, as a tiny girl curled into a ball and prayed for someone to come and kick her away. 'SHE'S FLAT! THIS ONE'S PRETTY MUCH DONE.'

No breasts for her. But not so for the early-blossoming next girl, who was probably already wearing what my grandmother used to call an 'over the shoulder boulder holder' and was probably very aware of it. And now, thanks to the A.B.S.G.N., so was everyone else. Including my dad, who had taken me for my fitting – probably expecting, as most sane people would have, that it would be done in a room somewhere, privately. The flowers may be delicate, but the gardeners rarely are.

Over the four years, we were expected to *fill that vest*. It wasn't like they would kick us out of school if we didn't – it was a silent expectation. The mountains would come to Mohammed (or Mary – Catholic school, after all). But once they were there, the school had very conflicted feelings about them. Cover them! Deal with them, girls, *they've arrived*! *They* were there, like some invaders from another planet we've always been grimly expecting.

I had to read the Bible cover to cover in school too, which contained passages such as this one, from the wise Solomon and his provocative Canticles – which I felt very well summarized our school's position as well:

> *We have a little sister*
> *who as yet has no breasts.*
> *What shall we do with our sister*
> *When she is asked in marriage?*
> *If she is a wall,*
> *We shall build on it a silver parapet;*
> *If she is a door,*
> *We shall bar it with a plank of cedarwood . . .*

I was one of those girls who never thought about the boob question much. I never really cared what size they were. I just shoved them into a bra in the morning and forgot about them. This, I suppose, is a luxury. Some people have massive ones that hurt their backs or keep them from seeing their shoes. Others feels inadequate. Mine were . . . enough? Basically there? I was much too busy trying to shred my indestructible polyester uniform and trying to understand the mysteries of Catholicism to care much about them. I had, in my opinion, Bigger Problems.

But I did notice that some people did care a lot, and I never quite grasped why. Why the attraction and shame and terror and pride. So much expectation and fuss over a few pounds (or ounces) of floppy meat and milk bag, as I would have sexily described them. And as an adult woman, I am excited to report I have never figured it out. I'm excited to write for a book about boobs, because it actually made me stop and wonder about the wonder.

And sure, the boobs are about as literal a symbol of life-giving power as you could hope to find. And the mixed range of emotions – lust, disgust, practical acceptance, comfort, annoyance – that the funbags contain within are certainly impressive. But in me, there is still an angry teenager in polyester who wants the freedom to take her shirt off in public, yet doesn't want the bother of dealing with the attention of taking her shirt off in public . . . who wants not to care about boobs. I'll get them mamogrammed and put them in a holder if I feel like it and feed a baby, but at the end of the day they are mine to ignore in favor of more interesting body parts. Like the hand. Or the head. Or the poor, undervalued spleen.

Perhaps the Amazing Breast-Size Guessing Nun actually gave me this gift of general apathy toward the entire subject, and for it, I thank her. For I am a field, and not a tower or a wall or a door. So are we all. And our flowers come in many sizes.

ALEX JONES

I used to be as flat as a pancake. While all the other girls secretly loved seeing the vague outline of their first bra through their blue school shirts, I was still sporting an M&S thermal vest. It was hell, and every night, without fail, I'd pray that I'd wake up with enough boobs to fill even an AA cup! Things hit an all-time low in Year Nine when I took to wearing a very stretchy elastic around my back so that there was something there that the boys could twang! Needless to say the only twang I felt was searing pain, having endured that tight elastic for seven long hours. In a nutshell, I was a violin-playing, 'boobless' geek. While some of the more 'developed' girls in Year Nine were complaining of sore boobs after netball practice (although, clearly exaggerating) I was only concerned with whipping my age 11–14 vest on and off quick enough in the changing rooms so that nobody would see my childlike body.

My boobs were late, as were my periods. I was stuck in perpetual girlhood waiting for life to begin. Then it happened. One beautiful morning at the end of June, circa 1994, a week or two after our GCSEs, I woke up and there they were. Two wonderful, fully grown breasts. I was officially a woman. Along came a well-needed dose of confidence and a posture change. There they were, two new friends who I'd waited so long for. And they grew and grew and grew. It was like the biggest 'boob explosion' of all time. I was finally blessed with a lovely pair of 30Es that I've treasured and loved dearly ever since. These days, they're not quite as pert as they once were, but we are working together to resist the pull of gravity. They're wrapped in a supportive sports bra during exercise, moisturised on a daily basis to try and ward off any stretch marks and ensconced comfortably in pretty underwear on my more organised days. They were a long time coming, but I've loved them every day since they arrived. They signalled becoming a woman and together, we have had a pretty exciting journey.

MARIAN KEYES

Years later, when I was all grown up, a friend told me that when she was a teenager she used to stuff her bra with tissues and I was both cheered and a bit miserable. At least someone else had been at it – but *tissues*! What difference would tissues make? Me? I had a pair of socks. In each cup.

Oh, it was terrible to be a flat-chested teenager!

Every teenage girl thinks their chest is too small (except for those few who fear theirs is too big) but mine really was non-existent. I looked like Iggy Pop. (See the cover of *Nude and Rude*.)

At fourteen I was full of yearning and longing and I was desperate for boys to fancy me. Breasts are very very powerful creatures, perhaps the most powerful things in the universe, and I had none. Also I felt my bum and thighs were way too big (they weren't) and I needed a proper chest to balance them out. I was *all wrong*.

Magazines urged me to do the pencil test – if you can hold a pencil between your breast and your ribcage, then it's time for a bra. I'd no idea what they meant. My boobs were like bee-stings. All the same, I found a pencil and gave it a go and watched the pencil fall to the floor. I tried again. And again. And eventually concluded there must be something wrong with the pencil.

If I'd been allowed to have a breast enlargement when I was sixteen, I'd probably have gone entirely overboard and done a Jordan on it. I'd have got them so big that I'd never have stood up straight again. But it was Ireland and it was 1980 and there was no such thing as breast augmentation back then. There weren't even padded bras.

So anyway, socks. Socks became my friends. Socks gave me the appearance of a chest. But it meant that I couldn't let anyone (read, boys) get too close.

When I landed a proper boyfriend things got awkward. He was keen to 'proceed' with matters and I was aware that there was a marked discrepancy between the boobs I had on view to the outside world and the boobs that were really there. I had to sit him down and say, in a serious talk sort of way, 'I have something to tell you.' I broke the dreadful news and I was mortified – but he wasn't a bit surprised. He'd known all along. Apparently socks don't have much bounce in them and it seemed I'd been a little delusional.

I knocked off the socks.

But still my boobs didn't grow. I came to the end of my teens and there was still no sign of them. And on into my twenties and still they stayed away. People told me I was a late developer, but I tried to make my peace with the fact that I'd be flat-chested forever.

Now and again I'd read a shock story about how every woman should get her chest measured because ninety-nine per cent of us don't wear the right bra size. Well I do, I thought gloomily. I was 32AA. We were all agreed on it. In fact I was afraid to be measured in case I transpired to be actually *smaller* than 32AA.

A well-meaning type told me how lucky I was to be flat-chested because when I got older I wouldn't have them swinging around my waist. I cannot tell you how little comfort this was to me at twenty-one.

Occasionally I'd read about girls who'd had to have operations to have their knockers reduced for health reasons, back pain and suchlike, and I'd be baffled – the ingratitude! Who cared about agony? I'd have been delighted with that sort of agony! Or those girls who complained that due to the size of their knockers, men only ever spoke to their chests, that they were objectified. Frankly, I'd have been *delighted* to be objectified!

But despite my abnormal flatchestedness, I did have boyfriends and eventually I even got married. In my early thirties suddenly I had a few quid and I could have afforded to have a breast enlargement and to my surprise I decided that actually I couldn't be bothered – I was fine as I was.

Then guess what happened – it turned out that I really *was* a late developer. Around the age of thirty-four, I suddenly grew boobs. I'm now a 36B. Okay, so I'm not Jordan, but would I want to be?

ANNIE MAC

Boobs, breasts, jugs, norks, mammary glands, whatever you called them, they were not welcome in my life. I spent my childhood years as a bona fide tomboy. I could climb all the trees down the green in my housing estate, I rolled with an all-boy skate crew, ollying my way up kerbs on my brother's old fibreglass skateboard, I played up front on the school football team, the only girl dribbling around the knobbly knees of a pitch full of pre-pubescent boys. I never dreamt of getting married, I never collected Barbie dolls, I was going to be a marine biologist or a set designer for the theatre when I grew up. Womanhood was an enigma, something I knew was inevitable but still very much a faraway mystery that would be solved YEARS down the line. Not until Tracey O'Connor took me into a toilet cubicle at lunchtime in 6th class and told me she had her period did the reality of impending puberty come crashing down on my happily oblivious existence. It was all hushed tones, talk of tampons and bleeding. Ominous stuff. Then we had the sex education class in school and I looked on, confounded, struggling to equate my body with the biological model of a cervix that was in front of me. I chose to ignore it all . . . until I came home from school one day to find my mother waiting for me in the kitchen with a book explaining sex. I burst out crying and ran out of the room. That's how I felt about sex at eleven. Two words. Not Ready.

The boobs came around the age of fourteen. There was the purchase of sports bras, worn as social armour, as a sign to say, 'Look! I'm grown up!' rather than out of any necessity. There was nothing there to support. Eventually, when my breasts started to grow, they grew lopsided. My left breast was noticeably bigger than my right. There were many traumatic hours stood in front of the mirror with my hands above my head, desperately willing my right breast to grow more. Oh what a turbulent and heightened time those early teens are, with everything growing out and up. I thought I was the only person in the world going through all this profound confusion; I was going to have lopsided breasts for the rest of my life!

My bathroom pleas were granted and my breasts finally balanced out. As the school years edged by and my skirt length edged up, they felt the crude groping hand movements of my various boyfriends. With a sex life came a pale pink box with the word 'Celeste' written across the front in delicate lilac letters. The contraceptive pill resulted in inexplicable mood swings. In tandem with the tears and turmoil there was the rapid and rather alarming swell of my breasts. A whole cup size in a matter of weeks! I went on and off the pill throughout my twenties and my breasts ballooned in and out, inflating and deflating in direct correlation to my sexual experiences.

Mid-twenties, a serious relationship and my first attempt at cohabitation meant routine and regular exercise for the first time in my life. I lost all my puppy fat and became a streamlined version of my previous pot-bellied self. My breasts shrank and have remained a very normal 34C, until now. Now, my body has changed wholly and completely. A blue cross on a white stick five months ago means I have become a vehicle. A tiny wriggly thing, fists clenched, eyes squeezed shut, is squirming in my uterus. I can feel it kicking. My belly is stretched and taut, my breasts swollen into huge fleshy pendulous receptacles, and my mind boggles with the miracle of my physiology. They are going to feed my baby. My own breasts are going to feed my baby. It is yet another chapter for them and me to get through. When I write it all down, they tell my story very well.

Some Girls Are Bigger Than Others

SARRA MANNING

It was meant to be a summer full of boys. The ones who worked at the funfair on the pier, their tans deepening as the weather got hotter and they took off their T-shirts to spin squealing, sunburnt kids on the Waltzers. The packs of guys down for the weekend to our dreary little seaside town, who wanted to steal kisses behind the amusement arcade. The boys from school who'd suddenly got taller and fitter and learned how to look at you as if you were the only girl in the world.

Which was why me and Jules had got summer jobs at the ice-cream parlour on the pier. Before my dad left we used to spend two weeks in Magaluf so my parents could hurl insults at each other in a Mediterranean setting. But now money was tight and if I had to spend summer at home then I needed to be where the boy action was. And when we turned up the first day in our matching white short shorts, the owner, Big Don, increased our pay to £5.50 an hour and all the sprinkles we could eat.

Yeah, it was going to be the best summer ever. And then three things fucked it completely and utterly up. Jules got appendicitis and was rushed to hospital. Her parents were so relieved that she didn't die that they took her off to Fuente Vera to convalesce. And Jules asked Louise to go with her because I'd insisted her stomach pain was trapped wind. Also I look way better in a bikini than her.

Then it started to rain and never stopped. The skies were permanently dark and the sea was an angry, bubbling grey cauldron. Big Don wasn't too bothered that his only customers were geriatrics making a small vanilla cone last an hour while they waited for the rain to die down to a light drizzle, but I was devastated at the lack of cute boys coming in for a Cornetto.

Then the summer went from sucking to officially sucking like no summer had ever sucked before. Because one morning there was Rosie cowering under the parlour's jaunty awning when I arrived to open up.

'Oh, hi, I'm Rosie,' she whispered so quietly I could barely hear her over the relentless drip-drip of the rain.

'Cath,' I said, giving the door a hard shove because it tended to stick. She was looking at me funny because we'd been at junior school together, but Rosie had gone on to the posh girls' school and she was wearing mum jeans and it seemed easier to pretend that I didn't know her.

But she was still the same quiet Rosie who crept round the edges. She looked around the ice-cream parlour nervously, as if she expected the metal scoops to spring to life and start attacking her. I opened the store cupboard and grabbed a handful of yellow cotton.

'Here, put this on,' I ordered. 'Loo's over there.'

Rosie reached out to catch her regulation 'I Scream, You Scream, We All Scream For Ice Cream' T-shirt, and I realised that she had changed. I mean, she was still small and round and her messy, mousy hair still obscured her pink cheeks, but Rosie *had* grown up. Or at least her breasts had. They were *huge*. And when she emerged from the bathroom in the figure-hugging T-shirt, her tits entered the room half an hour before she did. Large breasts were wasted on a girl like Rosie.

'It's a little bit tight,' she bleated forlornly, staring down at her chest in dismay.

'Yeah, sucks to be you.' She'd bogarted all the breastage so no way was she getting any sympathy from me. Then I launched into her orientation. 'It's pretty easy to figure out, apart from when someone wants to build their own sundae,' I finished. Rosie nodded and waited at the counter eagerly like we were about to be besieged by hungry customers.

Surprisingly we settled into a comfortable routine over the next few days. I'd serve if a hot guy came in but the pickings were pretty slim and I always got the mint choc chip and the pistachio mixed up. Rosie had way more patience at dealing with people and when it wasn't raining, she actually volunteered to hand out flyers because she was a loser.

But mostly I sat reading magazines and Rosie sat reading books. Proper books with tiny letters and fugly paintings on the front of girls who looked all swirly and watery.

We didn't talk at all. Until the day the guy who worked on the face-painting booth came in for a sundae. I rushed to serve him because he was under fifty and passably fit apart from the whole geek chic thing with his hipster specs and Jack Purcells and, OMG, a *cardigan*, but Rosie was already brandishing one of the scoops purposefully.

I watched in amazement as he took the Build Your Own Sundae promotion to scary places that it was never meant to go. Chocolate ice cream, double chocolate ice cream, chocolate fudge ice cream with chocolate sauce and a Flake was against all laws of God and WeightWatchers.

'I saw you handing out flyers this morning,' he remarked to Rosie, who blushed more furiously than usual. Boys probably didn't talk to her that much, except to comment on her mammoth appendages. 'I could take some for the face-painting booth if you wanted.'

Rosie did want. She wanted so badly that she even gave him an extra helping of chocolate sauce.

'Do you fancy him?' I asked when he'd left with his sundae perched precariously in one hand as he shifted the box of flyers under his other arm.

'I fancy not handing out flyers in a sudden downpour,' Rosie muttered. Her voice dropped. "Sides, boys like that don't fancy girls like me.'

'What, dorky boys in cardigans?'

'Whippet thin, arty boys with a casual insouciance,' Rosie said, which seemed like brainiac speak for dork. It also seemed like we'd used up our allotted word quota for the day.

I soon realised that Rosie really didn't like me. Like, she would never speak to me about anything not ice cream related. She'd either bury her head in one of her boring books or willingly serve customers without waiting for them to cough pointedly first.

I tried everything. I asked her about music but she only liked whiny emo bands. I asked her about her favourite TV shows but she was a freak who didn't have her own TV. By the time I asked her what her favourite colour was, I was officially desperate, but she just mumbled, 'green', as Cardigan Boy walked in.

He stood there trying to catch Rosie's eye but she was steadfastly gazing at the syrup bottles until I gave her a theatrical nudge. 'I don't serve dorks, so he's all yours,' I drawled.

If I'd been Rosie, I'd have engaged in some flirty talk involving the word 'vanilla', but Rosie just waited silently until Cardigan Boy decided on a praline and peanut butter combo. She dropped the first scoop on the floor and because I'm a saint, I offered to mop it up, while she tried again. Her legs were totally shaking and when I finally straightened up it was in time to hear him say, 'Nice badge,' as Rosie handed him his change.

The door had barely had time to close behind him, before she burst into tears.

Rosie wouldn't say why she was crying. She just ran into the loo. When she came out, her eyes were pink, like she'd been scrubbing at them with the scratchy toilet tissue that Big Don got from the cash and carry instead of the posh stuff we had at home.

'Are you all right?' I asked, but Rosie simply sniffed a bit and picked up her book.

It was much, much later when I'd just locked up and was gazing at the bulging sky and waiting for the first fat drops of rain to start plopping down, that Rosie spoke.

'I thought he was different,' she said, trying to yank the zip of her cagoule over her breasts. 'But he's the same as all the other boys.'

'He is different from other boys. He wears a cardigan, for God's sake.'

'No, I mean, it was just about these, wasn't it?' She gestured at her chest. 'He wasn't looking at my badge at all.'

I looked at her badge, which was hard because her breasts really were attention hoggers. 'Reading is sexy', it proclaimed, which it *so* wasn't, but if Cardigan Boy really had been looking at her badge and thought it was cool, then they were, like, kindred spirits or something.

'Maybe he was looking at your badge but your boobs are in the same area so he had to look at them too. They are kinda…'

'Big?' Rosie suggested coldly. 'Ginormous, don't get many of them to the pound, could have someone's eye out – whatever you were about to say, don't bother. I've heard it all before.'

'I was going to say gazeworthy,' I snapped because she could just get over herself. Lots of people would pay good money for a pair that weren't even half as impressive. 'How big are you anyway?' I heard myself asking. 'Like 40DD?'

'Oh, piss off,' Rosie hissed in a very un-Rosie-like manner and stomped off.

'I was only asking,' I pointed out, following her because I wanted to get off the pier before the heavens unleashed. 'Boys like boobs. Deal with it.' Which was precisely why I had a pair of rubber chicken fillets stuffed into my bra cups.

'Well, I like boys who can see beyond my chest to the person underneath,' Rosie muttered. 'If he doesn't like me for my personality then he's not worth it.'

'Do you want to know what your problem is, Rosie?'

'Apart from the way you keep haranguing me with rhetorical questions?' She folded her arms over the offending areas. 'What is my problem, oh wise one?'

'You think everything is about your breasts; but they wouldn't be so noticeable if you stopped tugging at your clothes and drawing attention to them every five seconds.' Rosie's hair was in her face and I couldn't tell whether my words were having any effect. 'You don't make the best of yourself. You should do something with your hair and stop letting your mum buy your clothes.'

'She doesn't buy my clothes . . .'

'Well, it looks like she does.' I tried to soften my voice because we were getting off topic. 'Look, Rosie, you might read lots of books but they're not teaching you important boy-getting life skills. Twenty-five per cent of your problem is obviously low self-esteem and the other seventy-five per cent of your problem will disappear if you let me work on your wardrobe, grooming and getting you a bra that actually fits.'

Rosie took the bait at last. 'What's wrong with my bra?'

I came right out with it. 'You have a mono-boob. There's meant to be two of them, not one long sausagey thing hanging there. I'm not a lezza or anything, Rosie, but I'd really love to know what's going on under your clothes.'

I hadn't even finished my sentence before Rosie bolted across the road and narrowly avoided getting mown down by a bus.

And that was that. If Rosie wanted to spend the rest of her life being a mono-boobed freak, it was nothing to do with me.

But three days later after Big Don had been in to give us our wages, Rosie sidled up as I stacked my magazines in a neat pile. 'It's late-night closing, isn't it? Will you help me buy some new bras?'

Rosie had a long list of acceptable behaviour for our bra-buying expedition. She refused to have her boobs measured. I wasn't allowed in the changing room. The words 'knockers', 'bristols', 'norks' and all other variants were banned and I wasn't to speculate on what her size might be.

I agreed to everything because even walking to the main shopping drag together was a big thing for Rosie. Acceptance was the first step to recovery, blah blah blah. And I almost shed a tear as I saw the light dawn on Rosie's face as I extolled the virtues of underwire bras and she snatched a handful and hurried to try them on. She was actually figuring out the basic rules of girl stuff before my very eyes.

When Rosie reappeared, and headed towards the cash register with her hands full of new bras and one greying old one, she was walking very oddly, as if her centre of gravity had totally shifted. Maybe it was because her boobs were no longer one weird roll propped on her chest, but like actual proper breasts. They were still enormous but at least they didn't look like they should have their own national anthem any more.

'You have a waist now,' I told her in amazement after she'd paid. 'You look super fierce.' I expected Rosie to give me another speech about how she only wanted to be judged for her lame personality, but a tiny, pleased smile played around her lips.

'I'm having this major epiphany,' Rosie confessed. 'I always thought it was superficial to care too much about clothes and hair and it was the inner me that counted. But maybe the outer me should look more like the inner me.'

She really needed to come with subtitles.

'What does the inner you look like,' I asked.

Turned out that Rosie's inner me looked like the girls in the books she read; quirky and mysterious, which I translated as a muted colour palette and lots of V-necks and wrap tops to minimise her mammaries. We trawled through New Look, Primark and H&M and Rosie tried on everything I suggested. I wouldn't say we were becoming friends, more like teacher and pupil.

Every day the skies got darker and the rain got more biblical and we'd camp out in one of the booths, so I could impart all the wisdom I'd acquired in my sixteen years.

Rosie took notes and when I was done imparting she made me laugh by inventing this whole other life for Big Don where he ordered girlfriends off the internet. She was dead sarcastic and funny once you got to know her.

There were hardly ever any customers but when Cardigan Boy came in, Rosie would hide from view and whisper: 'You serve him, Cath, please.'

But on Thursday when the bell above the door jangled I'd just given my nails their second coat of The Lady Is A Tramp, so with a long-suffering sigh, Rosie hauled herself up.

'Hey, I haven't seen you for ages,' he said and she almost tripped over her feet.

Then his eyes widened at new improved Rosie in a black V-neck sweater that fitted properly with a little felt corsage pinned to her shoulder and a pair of jeans that didn't give her a mum bum. And game on, because Cardigan Boy was looking at Rosie in exactly the same way that he'd looked at his Tropical Fruits sundae. Mind you, he'd looked at her like that pre-makeover too.

'I hope this doesn't sound sketchy, but I've got something for you,' he said nervously, reaching into the inner depths of his anorak while Rosie looked intrigued but nervous, because Cardigan Boy was coming over all stalker-y. 'I saw you reading *Bonjour Tristesse*, and then the other day I found this in a charity shop. You've probably already got it, but the cover's really cool.'

He pulled out a mouldy paperback, its pages tinged yellow. Rosie took it and turned it over carefully like it was some holy relic, as I squinted over her shoulder to see the book title: *To Esme, With Love And Squalor.* What*ever*. But Rosie's face lit up and in that split second she was so beautiful that it made me blink rapidly until she looked like she usually did.

'That's so weird, this is on my to-buy list,' she said. 'And I love old editions of books. If I really like the book, it makes me kinda sad that they gave it away. Do you know what I mean?'

Cardigan Boy knew exactly what she meant. 'I have this hardback of *The Collectible Dorothy Parker* from the 1940s that I found in Cancer Research. Why would someone get rid of that?'

It was all very well bonding over books but they still weren't getting the basics sorted. Not unless I did it for them. 'I'm Cath, this is Rosie and you are . . .?'

'David,' Cardigan Boy said. 'Never Dave or Davy or Id.'

And Rosie totally laughed, even though it was the lamest joke I'd ever heard. It was adorable in the dorkiest, geekiest way possible.

How was I going to get Rosie and David away from ice cream and on an actual date? I needed to try to fathom out the geek mindset but, God, that was so hard. Then on Tuesday Rosie was banging on about her latest boring book while I was flicking through the local paper and I had such a genius idea that I almost fell headfirst into the strawberry ice cream that I'd left out on the counter to soften.

When David finally came in, I elbowed Rosie out of the way, so I could get to him first. We went through the usual sundae business while he cast longing glances in Rosie's direction, then I moved in for the kill.

'Hey, have you ever read *The Great Gatsby*?' It was a perfectly natural question for me to ask so there was no need for him to smirk.

'It's one of my favourite books,' he replied and Rosie opened her mouth to start wordgasming about it too but I rustled the paper as a diversionary tactic.

'You know they made a non-musical film of it ages ago, right? It's playing at the Rep Cinema tonight.'

'I've always wanted to see it,' David enthused, walking into the clever trap I'd set and making himself right at home.

'Really?' I smiled sweetly at Rosie whose eyes were promising a little light torture. 'Rosie's dying to see it too but she hasn't got anyone to go with. I refuse to watch any film that wasn't made this century.'

If David paused for longer than five seconds I was going to brain him with a box of Cornettos, but he was already turning to Rosie with a casual smile that I knew masked the fear of rejection. 'You probably already have plans, but if you fancy going with me . . .?' He tailed off and stared down at his Jack Purcells. Which was just as well because Rosie was doing a good impression of a slack-jawed yokel.

'Um, if you don't mind, I guess that would be er, like all right,' she muttered.

'No, I don't mind. If you're sure you don't . . .'

It was like watching some nature show on the Discovery Channel about the mating habits of geeks. Watching two bears clawing each other into bloody shreds would have been less painful. 'Jesus!' I snapped, pushing his sundae at him. 'Come and pick her up after work. Six sharp so you've got time to get the tickets. Now go away. We might have some other customers in a minute.'

As soon as he was out of the door, Rosie turned on me furiously. 'You're absolutely unbelievable, Cath,' she began, her face flushing. 'You pimped me! He was obviously just being polite because you forced him into . . .'

'You're welcome,' I said when she had to pause for oxygen. 'If I were you I'd start doing your make-up because you're still crap at applying liquid eyeliner.'

'He paid extra for the superior comfort seats,' Rosie told me the next day, as we shivered behind the counter. It wasn't actually that cold but the rain was thudding against the window and it felt like we should shiver. 'And then we shared a tub of popcorn and he squeezed my arm in a really sad part of the movie, but it wasn't in a lecherous way. It was a very empathetic squeeze.'

'And then what happened?' I prompted, eyes wide.

'We went for a coffee and talked about the movie and Scott

115

Fitzgerald's other books, and loads of things and then he walked me home,' Rosie finished with a smile that was verging on smug.

'And did he kiss you? Like, with tongues?' It came to something when I had to get vicarious snogging thrills from Rosie.

'Maybe he did, maybe he didn't,' she said coyly. 'But I'm seeing him tonight. We're going to a gig. You should come,' she offered, because she was a sweet but totally naïve girl who thought it was polite to invite friends along on dates.

'Nah, you're OK,' I shrugged. 'The music you like hurts when you listen to it.'

'Some of David's friends are going to be there.' Rosie's face squinched up. 'Maybe they won't like me. They're all at university or art school and they'll think that I'm fat . . .'

'You are not fat,' I interrupted angrily because at least she didn't go straight up and down like me. 'You're curvy. Big diff. And you're really smart and funny and you should stop judging yourself about what you think you look like. It's pathetic. And don't you forget it.'

Rosie didn't forget it. Maybe that's why she was a such big hit with David's friends. She even went bowling with them later in the week, then turned up for work in this old-fashioned dress that hugged her curves like she'd just stepped down from one of those 1950s pin-up girl pictures. Her boobs were still mighty but it was like she'd grown into them.

'David's friend Kara gave me this,' she said, twirling so I could see how the circle skirt foofed out. 'She said I had the perfect figure for vintage clothes.'

I was happy for her. Really I was. That's why I folded my

arms and pouted. 'You could get something in H&M that's practically identical,' I noted savagely. 'And no one would have died in it.'

Rosie's face fell and I felt like a bitch for raining all over her vintage parade, but I could tell she was leaving me behind and there wasn't a thing I could do about it.

We still hung out at work but it wasn't the same. Rosie was kicking it freestyle these days and now that I had nothing left to teach her, there wasn't really a lot to talk about.

So it was a huge relief when it stopped raining and the sun came out. Big Don dragged the Mr Whippy machine outside to take advantage of the daytrippers and I volunteered to man it. I couldn't quite master the necessary twirling action but I really needed to start on my tan and scope out the talent.

The sunshine had made the boys emerge from wherever they'd been hiding and I remembered what summer was meant to be about. I'd lost too much time for sticky kisses and holding hands with out-of-towners. I needed to think about who'd still be around in September when everyone at school was bragging about Pedro the cabana boy and François the deckchair salesman. If I had a boy in the bank, so to speak, rather than living off memories, then I wouldn't need any sympathetic looks because newly one-parent families couldn't afford luxuries like package holidays to Corfu.

First I considered Jimmy from the Waltzers because he was really fit, but he had dirty fingernails and everyone knew he'd done really gross stuff with a girl from the doughnut stall under the pier. Loz from the Ghost Train always winked at me when he came to beg for change, but he had a zitty back and he spent off-season in a spliff haze. I needed a boy who was way more thrusting and dynamic.

Eventually I settled on Kieran from the bumper cars because he played football for the local club's youth team, drove a black Jeep, and when he sauntered bare-chested along the pier with a cocky smile, his muscles rippled and it was like having a religious vision. He was perfect for me.

I pulled out every single weapon in my arsenal. I went two shades lighter on the blonde scale, fashioned my T-shirt into a bandeau to show more skin and smiled flirtatiously every time he walked past. Nothing seemed to work, and the skanks from the café opposite had set up a tea stall outside the front door and weren't above whistling at him. I could have been invisible for all the notice Kieran took of me.

Summer was limping to a halt and I could feel the weight of going back to school already crushing down on me. I needed a Plan B on the boy front, I thought as I served up 99 after 99. And as soon as I thought it, a voice in my ear roughly enquired, 'You all right, then?'

It was Kieran. I mean, of course it was Kieran, and all of him was twinkling at me: his eyes, his smile, the bleached tips of his spiky hair. I stuck out my chest and fluttered my eyelashes. 'Yeah,' I said, staring at his mouth. 'You all right?'

'You're Cath, right?' Kieran asked and I forgot the impatient queue of customers and the girls from the café trying to kill me with their collective dirty looks. Because Kieran was all there was and his eyes were running up my legs, over my tummy, lingering slightly at the boobs then coming to rest on my mouth as I poked my tongue slightly between my lips like I was deep in thought.

'Yeah,' I said after about five seconds. 'And you're Kieran. Your cousin knows my mate, Jules.'

'So, like, do you want to go to the Pier Summer Party with me on Friday?'

I had to stop myself from squealing because we were so *on*. Every summer, the business owners who rented space on the pier held a party for their under-paid, over-worked summer staff. It was at some cheesy club in town but it was just about the most exciting event of the season. And Kieran wanted to walk in with me in full view of those jealous ho-bags from the café who'd taken to shouting rude remarks at me in their quiet periods. Result!

'Sure, that sounds cool,' I said casually as Kieran asked for my number. And it was that easy to get the guy you fancied – if you weren't Rosie.

I was in torment most of Friday as I tried to dish up ice cream and beautify myself. There was a hairy moment when I spilled a glob of body shimmer in the chocolate chip but I smooshed it around with a scoop and I don't think anyone noticed. Well, only Rosie and she didn't count.

Once we'd finally closed and I was carefully applying glittery eye-shadow, I saw her mardy reflection in my compact. 'Rosie, you are going to this party, right?' I asked suddenly, because I hadn't thought to check.

'Why would I willingly spend time in a room full of people I'd normally cross the road to avoid?' Rosie said, though a simple 'no' would have done. 'It's not my scene.'

'But you have to come!' I yelped, closing my compact with a snap and fiddling with the neckline of my dress so it didn't dip down low enough to reveal my darkest secrets. 'Is David going?'

'It's not his scene either,' Rosie sniffed, like they were too good to get down and dance to songs that had an actual tune. 'Anyway, you're going with Kieran, so what's the problem?'

How could Rosie not know this stuff? 'Because I don't want him to think I'm some friendless loser who spends the entire night clinging to him,' I all but wailed. 'Look, just come for a couple of hours.'

'I can't,' Rosie said firmly. I'd preferred her when she'd been a total pushover and had no social life to interfere with my plans. 'We're going to see a band and we have to catch a train and –'

'God, I can't believe you're one of those girls who dumps your mates as soon as you get a boyfriend,' I burst out. 'You wouldn't even have hooked up with him if it hadn't been for me.'

'That's not fair,' Rosie protested, her voice throbbing like she was getting teary. But she was still picking up her bag like she intended to abandon me. 'That's a really unkind thing to say, Cath.'

I was about to say a lot more really unkind things when there was a tap on the window and I whirled around to see Kieran raise a hand and shoot me one of those wolfish smiles, which made my knees shake. 'Oh, why don't you just go home and read one of your mouldy books,' I hissed. 'That's the closest you'll ever come to having a life.'

'I can't believe that I actually thought you were my friend,' Rosie choked as she hurried to the door and almost knocked Kieran off his feet. And he could take his eyes off her tits too.

'We were never friends,' I stated clearly. 'I just felt sorry for you.' And before Rosie could put a complete damper on the evening and to get Kieran's attention away from her scene-stealing mammaries, I dragged him down for a long, tongue-y kiss until she was just a fat, round blob in the distance.

The party was fantastic. When I walked in with Kieran, everyone turned to look at us like we were this golden couple or something. I kept a tight hold of Kieran's hand and maybe it was that and the kiss we'd had before that made him so, like, demonstrative.

'You're so hot, Cath,' he kept saying, while rubbing his hand against whatever part of my body was nearest. 'You're the fittest girl here.'

Technically I wasn't, because Lizzie who worked on the rock stall had got through to the semi-finals of this TV modelling competition, but whatever. Kieran was totally acting like we were officially dating and kept the Barcardi Breezers coming. And he only let me leave his side to go to the loos, where I adjusted the fillets and applied more body shimmer to give me the illusion of cleavage. When I got back to the bar, Kieran was hemmed in on all sides by those cows from the café. I staggered over so I could simultaneously wrap myself around Kieran and shoot death stares at them.

The party was winding down by then and Kieran and I ended up on a sofa at the back of the upstairs bar. Normally I don't like getting off with someone in public but it was dark and there wasn't much to see; just Kieran sprawled out on top of me while he tried to hump my leg. It reminded me of the fight between my mum and dad when she'd taken the dog to the vets to have his balls chopped off. The dog, not my dad. And I was so busy thinking about castration and poor old Muttley that I wasn't paying any attention to where Kieran's hands were going, which was straight into my bra cups.

'What the fuck is that?' he muttered in my ear and before I could process the full horror of the moment, he'd yanked out one of my rubber fillets and was staring at it in bemusement.

'S'nothing!'

I tried to make a grab for it but Kieran was already jack-knifing off the sofa so he could look down and see one breast all perky and firm while on the other side there was nothing but gaping material. He laughed. He actually laughed. 'Are you really a girl, Cath, or are you just a bloke in a dress?'

'Give it back!' I squealed, trying to make a lunge for him, but he took a hasty step back and I fell off the sofa and landed in a heap on the floor. Which would have been Kieran's cue to apologise, scoop me up in his arms and kiss me better.

He didn't. Kieran just gave the chicken fillet a tentative prod and sniggered again. 'I heard you were tight and now I know why.'

OK, Kieran wasn't the most sensitive specimen that boykind had to offer, but I've always had a weakness for the rugged bad boys. So I should have known what would happen as Kieran's pack of bumper-car mates tripped up the stairs.

'Look what Cath was packing under her dress,' he shouted, as he threw the fillet at them.

I cried the whole way home. And then my mum wanted to know what had happened and when I told her she said that all men were bastards, then *she* started to cry, which made me cry even harder. Then I cried because I'd ripped my new Zara dress and I missed my dad and there was no one to say that it would be all right because nothing was going to be all right ever again. Not until I got my new boobs and I met some rich guy who'd take me away from this stinking town and everyone in it and I never had to come back.

In fact, I spent most of the night crying, when I wasn't throwing up, and the next morning I really wanted to call in sick. But I had a new appreciation for my £5.50 an hour and the bigger boobs it would buy me so I stuck on my fake Gucci shades and my longest skirt, which just skimmed my knees, and staggered to work.

Rosie was already waiting for me to open up and I just couldn't deal with her right then. Especially as the first words out of her mouth was, 'You were vile last night.'

'Don't talk to me,' I spat and tried to ignore the way her face sort of collapsed in on itself. It was raining again, which suited me just fine because sunny skies would have made my head hurt even worse. I sat at the counter and ignored Rosie. By some sheer feat of inner strength that I didn't know I possessed, I managed not to cry for a few hours. Not even when some cow started moaning about the chocolate-chip ice cream tasting funny. I scooped and assembled cones and asked people if they wanted 'sprinkles or sauce?' in a drone-like voice.

I just needed to last until six and then I could go home and go to bed and cry a bit more but time had slowed down to a crawl and there were still two hours until I could herd the last ice-cream guzzlers out of the shop. I stared at the clock on my phone, then gave a little start as it beeped. Then I gave an even bigger start when I saw that I had a text from Kieran.

It was a bit late to apologise but *at least* he was apologising. That was something. I eagerly opened the message and then I really did burst into tears and six o'clock be damned. Once I started crying I couldn't stop and was only dimly aware of someone guiding me into the storeroom where they sat me down and tried to dab at my face with a damp tissue.

It took a long while for the sobs to die down to hiccups and Rosie was still crouched down in front of me with a concerned expression on her face.

'What about the shop?' I spluttered.

Rosie shrugged carelessly. 'I put the "back in five minutes" sign up on the door about half an hour ago,' she said breezily as if Big Don's profit margins weren't her problem. 'Is this about Kieran? What's he done?'

I tried to explain what had happened but every time I opened my mouth, a fresh volley of sobs emerged. In the end I handed over my phone so she could see the picture of my rubber fillet stuck to a wall and the text: 'Feel like chicken tonight? Call Cath on 077557 . . .'

She gave a little gasp, stared fleetingly at my chest, which was as flat as my mood, and then narrowed her eyes. 'I knew he was no good,' Rosie announced. 'You can't trust a boy who bleaches his hair. It shows a lack of character.'

It was such a Rosie thing to say that I actually smiled. Until I looked at my phone and my face crumpled again. 'I bet he's sent it to everyone in his address book and they'll have sent it to everyone in their address book.' I hunched over as the enormity of the situation dawned on me. 'I'm going to be a flat-chested freak of a laughing stock. Oh God, it will be all round school too. This must be how Kim Kardashian felt when her sex tape got leaked.'

There was nothing else to say so I decided to start crying again.

She totally didn't have to, but Rosie was really cool about it. She let me skulk in the storeroom so I could come up with a convincing argument to persuade my mum to get a bank loan so I could have my surgery before I went back to school. Then I could pretend that the rubber fillets weren't mine and also start a vicious rumour that Kieran wore a codpiece. It was a long shot, but it might just work.

My musings were interrupted by a knock on the storeroom door, which burst open to reveal Kieran standing there, Rosie's hand around his wrist in a vice-like grip, if the ouchy expression on Kieran's face was anything to go by.

'I can take it from here,' she called out and over her shoulder I saw David and a couple of face-painting-booth geeks fade into the distance. 'Kieran has something he wants to say to you,' Rosie told me in a sing-song voice and I couldn't understand why Kieran was letting her treat him like a bitch until she did something with her nails and his wrist that made him yelp like the spineless wanker that he really and truly was.

I lifted up my blotchy face and wished that I still had my shades on. 'What could you possibly want to say to me?' I asked dully.

'I'm sorry,' he spat sullenly.

'Why don't we try that once again with more feeling?' Rosie suggested pleasantly. 'Like we discussed after David threw your phone off the end of the pier. Or I'm digging my nails in again, and I don't care if it is your throwing arm.'

'I'm sorry that I acted like a Nean . . . like a Nean-der . . . like a tool last night. It was really disrespectful of me to treat you so objectively and . . .' Kieran faltered and Rosie hissed something in his ear. 'I need to appreciate women for their minds and not just their individual physical attributes.' He broke off from the script to shoot me a reproachful look. 'I was only having a laugh, Cath. Why you being so touchy about it?'

'Because you humiliated me in front of all your friends,' I hissed. 'And I bet you sent that text to everyone on the south coast and now I'm going to have to be home-schooled or something.'

Rosie let go of Kieran, who rubbed the back of his hand and flushed. 'Actually I ran out of credit after I sent you that text,' he admitted. 'I didn't send it to no one else, I swear. And I don't mind that you've got no tits, I still fancy you.'

The huge wave of relief swept away everything else in its path. But if there was a footballer in my future who'd lead me by the hand to a world where I was special and important and there was a never-ending supply of designer handbags and spa memberships, it wasn't Kieran.

'Well, I don't fancy you,' I confessed flatly. 'Not any more. Not after what you did.'

He stumbled out after that, mumbling something indistinct, though the word 'bitch' was loud and clear. Rosie raised her eyebrows at me and sort of shrugged.

'Thanks,' I said, even though it was really inadequate because she'd just saved my life.

But Rosie seemed to understand because she gathered up my bag and shades. 'Come on, let's get out of here,' she said decisively. 'You need junk food.'

It wasn't until I was tucking into a huge basket of fries in the nearest pub that didn't ask for ID that Rosie remembered to text David to let him know I wasn't going to top myself or anything. I felt a pang of envy because when would it be my turn to have a devoted boyfriend?

'See, it's stuff like this whole Kieran business which is exactly why I've spent my summer dishing up ice cream so I can save to get my tits done,' I blurted out before chugging down a whole glass of Diet Coke because I was never drinking alcohol again, not even when I was eighteen and legally old enough.

Props to Rosie because she didn't chew me out for letting her rattle on about her own breast issues without ever fessing up. 'Maybe it's not your tits that's the problem, maybe it's the guys you go for,' she said mildly.

That was so typical of her! 'I can't help if it I'm genetically programmed to only fancy boys who want the whole package; blonde hair, long legs, big boobs.'

'But you said it was all about confidence,' Rosie pointed out. She was starting to sound a little peeved. 'That I should stop worrying about what other people thought of me.'

'Well, maybe I kinda lied,' I admitted. 'Confidence only gets you through the door – doesn't get you into the VIP room though.'

Rosie threw her hands in the air like I was getting on her last nerve. 'You know if you used your powers for good, not evil, you could totally eradicate world hunger in six months,' she said, as she pinched one of my fries. 'Seriously, Cath, don't you think if you stopped concentrating on making your hair super shiny and chatting up creepy boys, you could use all that determination to do anything you wanted?'

'But all I want is to have super-shiny hair and actual breasts so I can attract a really cute boy with lots of money who'll take me away from this shitty little place,' I said round a mouthful of hot potato. 'Ain't gonna happen any other way.'

'Well, you could study hard, go to university and get a really well-paid job,' Rosie suggested, but my face scrunched up because I was that close to crying again.

'That would take way too long,' I moaned. 'And I'd make an ace trophy girlfriend . . .'

Rosie's eyebrows shot up so high that I thought she'd need surgery to remove them from her hairline. 'You have to figure out who you really want to be, then make sure the people in your life are going to help you achieve that. Like you helped me see beyond my 36Fs.'

It wasn't that simple but now I was distracted by Rosie's true bra size. 36F? F? How could such a thing be possible when I was a 32AA? Before I could ask Rosie, she was digging in her bag and pulling out a notebook and pen.

'You need a proper plan for the future,' she said firmly. 'One that doesn't involve invasive surgery.'

'You sound like my careers advisor, except he thinks my only future is working in a call centre,' I grumbled.

Rosie ignored my whining and held her pen poised over a snowy-white page. 'You're very goal orientated, love a challenge and we're going to come up with a project to make the most of that potential. Now, what do you really want to be when you grow up? And if you say footballer's wife, I'm going to smack you.'

'We'll keep in touch,' Rosie insisted on our last day when we were helping Big Don out by eating our way through the last of the Flakes. 'I'm still going to need tons of fashion advice.'

But we weren't and she wouldn't. Rosie had her own sense of style now and she was doing a gazillion A-levels and had plans to visit David in London. While I'd be stuck retaking the GCSE's I'd spectacularly failed, because it was hard to revise when your parents were throwing crockery at each other. Which was why I'd thrown her bullet-pointed list of my future goals and aspirations in the trash. And I was thinking about buying bigger boobs again because finding a rich boyfriend seemed more doable than ever passing English.

'Yeah, for sure,' I sighed, but Rosie didn't even notice my utter lack of conviction because she was dragging out a huge brown-paper parcel from the back of the storeroom.

'I prepared some audio-visual aids for your project,' she said, thrusting it into my hands and smirking when I nearly collapsed under the weight. 'No peeking until you get home.'

When I got home my mum was well into the first bottle of wine of the evening so I carried the package upstairs and ripped into it. I sifted through the collection of CDs and yellowing books that smelt of damp until I found a note written in Rosie's crabbed scrawl.

Dear Cath

Before I met you, these were the people who showed me that there's a whole big world out there and that who I am isn't who I'm always going to be. I hope they do the same for you.

Love Rosie

It was really sweet of her, but I wasn't Rosie. We were completely different people. Like, the huge diff in our breast sizes wasn't a big enough clue. I shoved the package to one side and then Jules called me and I forgot about it.

I kept forgetting about it until one night in October when there was nothing on TV and I'd just dumped another lad from the school football team because he only spoke in grunts. I groped about under the bed and pulled out the first book from the package I could reach: *Madame Bovary* by some bloke called Gustave Flaubert.

I took a deep breath, turned to the first page and began to read.

DAVINA MCCALL

I have always had a real love of breasts. Mammalian protuberances, lills, jugs, tits, funbags, boobs . . . so many words for two lovely mounds.

I am conscious of the fact that there may be some people reading this with eyebrows raised, a bit worried about what's happened to me. I must be long overdue for some sort of hugely public breakdown. Could this be it? Well, I'm afraid the answer is emphatically NO. I have a perfectly sane reason for my enormous respect and love for breasts, and here it is.

A long long time ago, when Showaddywaddy were a band and tinned ravioli was a luxury, I went on holiday with my mum. This in itself is a story. But I'll save that for the autobiography that I will never write.

Going on holiday with my mum was rare. I would often visit her in Paris but going on holiday WITH her . . . very rare. Primarily because I really cramped her style and was a hindrance to her partying. No judgement – she was very young and beautiful and drank a lot and wanted to party.

So I loved/loathed these trips. I would have way more free rein than at home, could eat whatever I wanted, stay up mega late and wander off and she never really noticed . . . but all I really wanted was for her to notice, and be a mummy . . . a cuddly mummy that would hold a towel up for me when I got out of the pool.

This is not a sob story by the way . . . just how it was, and relevant to my boob love.

So there I was, seven or eight years old, in the sea, tippy-toe depth, no one watching, swimming non-stop underwater – my nickname was shark. I was an awesome swimmer and I could stay under for an eternity. I took a dive down, swimming along, left it till the very last moment and came up for air just as a Hobie Cat sailboat came by and hit me on the head.

It knocked the stuffing out of me. I swallowed an ocean of water and got thrown around. The next thing I know two hands are lifting me up, head above water.

I gasp, coughing and crying all at the same time, and this lovely cuddly lady holds me so tight I go limp. I feel safe. My head in her chest, resting on her lovely safe boobs.

She felt like a mummy. A really, really lovely mummy. I didn't want to let go but as we got into shallower water she couldn't lift me any more. I said thank you and ran to find Mummy.

After much searching there she was, but by the time I'd found her I'd calmed down. I knew if I told her it wouldn't achieve anything, so I didn't bother.

I will never forget that kind lady, and ever since then I have had a great love of breasts and the comfort they can bring, in so many different ways.

And I always hold the towel up for my kids.

Twenty Things I Love About My Boobs

SARAH MILLICAN

1. They didn't turn up until I left school so no boys ever got to snap my bra strap. It's very hard to twang a vest.

2. They catch cake crumbs. Like nature's bib.

3. I keep my pencils under there.

4. They stop men calling me 'mate' on the bus. (I used to get called 'son' a lot as a kid but that might have been the hair).

5. They help you learn the alphabet. I know up to H.

6. Mine make a good warm pillow for kittens and boyfriends.

7. I once cheered up a sad friend by flashing my boobs and she laughed (from the surprise, I like to think).

8. They are the bridge between 'just kissing' and 'thank God I've shaved me legs cos we're doing it!"

9. They save me from suffocation. (I sleep on my stomach and they stop me from lying too flat.)

10. They're like a built-in bumper. It would be hard to crack a rib with these babies on duty.

11. My boyfriend says they make lovely hand warmers.

12. They are the reason I don't really want to lose weight. (I'll be left with just a gut rather than curves.)

13. The best time of any day is when I take my bra off. Whether I'm at home, on a train, in a cinema or driving (always pull in to release the beasts. Safety first. Comfort second).

14. Motorboating, where someone you know (preferably) puts their face betwixt your knockers and makes the noise of a small engine, can be used as self defence (depending on the size of the boobs and assailant).

15. In a good bra, they make me feel like a 1950s Hollywood starlet.

16. In a certain nightie, I look like Bubbles DeVere. But, wow, is that nightie comfy.

17. In bed, they keep my underarms warm.

18. They can accidentally click a link on my laptop.

19. Their size means I can't see my belly. Therefore it mustn't exist.

20. Underneath them is the first place I get sweaty. A sign to turn the heating down. Like a woozy canary in a mine.

The Ticking Clock

LEE MONROE

'Now, just pop your blouse off, and let's examine your breasts.'

Phoebe stiffened. 'It's OK,' she began. 'I know . . .'

The nurse smiled and Phoebe's eyes dropped to the woman's chest. One buttonhole stretching slightly in her shirt. A glimpse of off-white lace. The nurse's breasts were big. A couple of small melons, equally sized, if drooping a little under their weight.

'You know how to examine your own breasts?'

Phoebe nodded. The truth was she had only a vague idea of self-examination. It freaked her out to touch herself like that. Her breasts freaked her out. Small and not as firm as they should be, like two old golf balls past their best. Considering she was only seventeen, this seemed to Phoebe odd and cruel. If they were this dismal now, what would they be like when she was thirty?

Phoebe shuddered inside. She looked into the nurse's eyes and blinked.

'Try and relax,' said the nurse. 'I've seen all shapes and sizes, sweetheart, believe me.'

Phoebe tried to smile but she felt her heart thudding loudly. The nurse was trying to be reassuring, but she had never seen breasts like Phoebe's. No one had seen Phoebe's breasts. She made sure of that.

She'd only come to see the nurse to give a urine sample. Her cystitis was back again. But apparently you had to be subjected to a thorough examination these days. Trapped in a small white-walled office where a bed framed by a plastic curtain taunted you. Not to mention the posters on the walls, illustrating every possible disease a woman could be suffering from.

This was Phoebe's idea of hell.

On the desk behind them, the phone rang, loudly. Phoebe stepped back from the woman, hoping for a reprieve. But the nurse was still staring at her, unmoving, even though the phone kept on ringing behind her.

'Aren't you going to answer that?' Phoebe was breathless now. She stared at the phone. 'It might be an emergency . . .'

The nurse cocked her head to one side. So she wasn't stupid, Phoebe thought. She knew what Phoebe was up to. The moment seemed to go on for ever; the woman and the girl staring each other out. An impasse. Eventually, the nurse sighed and turned back to her desk and the phone. She moved towards it and picked up the receiver.

'Sandra Taylor,' she answered briskly, a little impatiently.

While Sandra's back was turned, Phoebe took the opportunity to look down at her shirt. A sheer drop, perhaps the hint of two small mounds. She glared at the view. Loathing herself.

The nurse was still talking, and lowering herself on to the

chair in front of the desk.

'I see,' she was saying, her voice dropping a little. 'Well, put her down on the list, I'll see her when I've finished with this one.'

Phoebe felt the prick of tears coming. Somehow being referred to this way just compounded the horror of this whole ordeal. On one level she knew she was being silly and weak. But she felt sick at the thought of anyone touching her. Feeling for themselves what a weird freak of nature she was.

Phoebe thought of Anna, her best friend. Anna had a strange-shaped bottom, and wide hips, no definition in her ankles. But her boobs. Her boobs were perfect. Evenly sized, round, bouncy. Womanly. Anna would be aghast if she could see Phoebe's terror now. Anna never wasted an opportunity to show off her tits. But Anna didn't, couldn't ever know, what it was like to have such hideous pockets of fat just sitting, useless on her chest. Anna would never know the shame that Phoebe felt every day.

Phoebe was approaching a panic attack. She was starting to sweat now. When she looked down at herself again, damp patches were spreading, under her arms, then spattering the midriff of her cotton shirt. Her neck was damp too. Her hairline. She concentrated on breathing out, keeping her eyes on Sandra's back. Sandra was still talking, scratching her head now. She seemed stressed. Phoebe felt hopeful. She slowly bent to pick up her jacket and eased it on. She buttoned it up over her damp shirt, already feeling calmer as she covered herself up. Phoebe picked up her bag and put it over her shoulder. It was heavy with all her school coursework. She breathed out. And in. And out again.

'Look, I'm with a patient now.' Sandra's voice was getting

louder. 'I'll see Mrs Evans when I've finished my booked appointments –' She sighed loudly, clearly interrupted by the voice on the other end of the call.

Phoebe cleared her throat and Sandra turned at the sound. She frowned and cupped her hand over the receiver.

'One moment,' she mouthed at Phoebe.

But Phoebe was already out of there. In her mind she was at the bus stop, waiting joyfully for the bus, ecstatic to be free.

'I'm sorry, I really have to go,' she said quickly, forcefully. 'I'm sorry.'

'Just a minute,' Sandra said firmly into the phone. 'I'll be with you in half a minute,' she told Phoebe.

'I'm sorry,' said Phoebe, already opening the door. 'I'll come back another time.'

And without waiting for Sandra's response, Phoebe fled.

Her mother was marking papers at the kitchen table when Phoebe arrived home. Phoebe's mum lectured in Politics at the university. She was deep in concentration, which suited Phoebe. She didn't want any questions. Not even about the cystitis.

Phoebe hung up her coat and filled the kettle. In its shiny metal she saw a distorted view of her shirt, creased now. The reflection made her chest look bigger. Like it might look if only she wasn't her. Phoebe. She looked away. The sound of the water boiling roused her mother.

'Sorry, Phoebs,' she said, sounding tired. 'How was your day?'

With her back to her mother, Phoebe smiled, glad of her

mum's absentmindedness.

'Fine,' she said quite happily. 'Same as usual really.'

She poured water into two mugs and added teabags. When she had made the drinks she turned and put a mug down in front of her mum. Her mother was yawning now, stretching.

'Thanks.' She picked up her tea and blew on it.

Phoebe shut her eyes, relaxing.

'Oh. What did the doctor say?' her mother asked, remembering.

Phoebe's eyes opened and she shrugged. 'I just gave a sample,' she said easily. 'I'll get the results back in a week or so.'

Her mum nodded, satisfied with the answer.

Phoebe looked momentarily at her mum's breasts. They were normal. She felt a surge of anger. Why were her mum's breasts normal-sized when hers were so pathetic and ugly?

'Mum?' she said, sitting down across from her. 'I want a breast enlargement.'

Her mother's eyes widened and she swallowed a mouthful of tea, putting her mug down carefully.

'I'm . . . Sorry, darling. Did you just say you wanted a breast enlargement?'

Phoebe nodded. She managed to keep the colour coming to her cheeks. Just saying that out loud felt shameful. Admitting the problem. But also shallow and ridiculous. Like a minor celebrity in *Heat* magazine. Phoebe's mother was staunchly progressive. A feminist. This would not go well. It would take all Phoebe's powers of persuasion. It would take a giant effort of manipulation.

But it would be worth it.

Her mother was studying her. She didn't look angry. A bit shocked, perhaps.

'Are you serious?' she said. She raised an eyebrow.

'I hate my breasts.' Phoebe's voice was remarkably calm. Saying it out loud had also brought more weight to her problem too.

Now she just needed to bring more weight to her pitiful mammary glands.

Her mother was shaking her head.

'But you have beautiful breasts,' she told Phoebe. 'You're a beautiful young woman.'

'You don't know,' Phoebe said quickly, panicked at being talked out of it now that she had decided. 'You haven't seen me naked in. . . . in, like six years.'

Her mother looked amused, and Phoebe felt annoyance ripple through her.

'Don't laugh, Mum. It's not funny.'

Her mother stopped smiling. She reached out and tried to take Phoebe's hand.

'Phoebe. You're seventeen. You're so young.'

But Phoebe put her hands in her lap, pushing them down through the gap in her thighs.

'Exactly. I should have the perfect body, shouldn't I, by now? I've stopped growing. I'm never going to have bigger tits.'

Her mother winced at the word 'tits'. She withdrew her hand, and stood up from the table. Then she walked out of the kitchen.

Phoebe slumped in her chair. Her mother had signalled the end of the conversation. Phoebe should never have said 'tits'. She'd gone about this all wrong. Silly and weak. Like her silly weak tits.

But then her mum returned, and she was holding an album. It was old. One Phoebe remembered from when she was small. She hadn't looked at it in years.

Her mum sat down. She pushed away her laptop and her papers and opened the album.

'Come over here,' she told Phoebe, quite gently.

Phoebe was in no mood to go down memory lane, but she rose and sat down on the chair next to her mother. She sighed heavily. Petulantly. Her mother pretended not to notice the moody teenager beside her. She leafed through a couple of the spreads in the album, but stopped at one, holding the album up so that they could both see it properly. She pointed at a picture of a girl in a bikini, sitting on the end of a jetty. Her blonde hair pulled back, wet from swimming. The girl was skinny, broad shouldered but pretty much flat-chested.

'That was taken in the south of France,' said her mother, wistfully. 'I was eighteen, and it was the first holiday I'd had without my parents.'

'Oh. Yes,' Phoebe didn't want to be pulled in to whatever trick this was, but she stared at the picture. Her mum looked very pretty, tanned and all limbs. Long legs, slender arms, slightly boyish, but undeniably attractive.

'So,' said Phoebe obtusely, after a pause. 'It's a nice picture, Mum.'

Her mother lowered the album.

'I didn't wear a bra in those days. I never felt I needed to. I

142

was quite convinced my breasts were never going to grow any bigger than they were then.'

Phoebe twitched. She didn't want to hear this.

'And then, a few years later, I was working as a teacher. It was my first year out of training and I wasn't having a very good time. School was difficult, I didn't feel I fitted in. The headteacher was strange around me. Awkward. I had no idea why, until one of the other teachers, Lynne – haven't seen her for years now – told me there were a few comments about me going around amongst the staff. Comments about my general "free and easy" way of dressing. Lynne told me . . .' Phoebe noticed her mother blushing. 'Barbara told me that my nipples were a particular source of interest. Or more accurately, disapproval. She told me I should think about buying a "decent" bra or two . . .'

Phoebe shared her mother's embarrassment. She bit her lip, cringing slightly.

'So,' her mother went on. 'I took myself off to Marks and Spencer and did a rather ill-informed dash around the underwear department. It was such an alien environment to me that I just took whatever bra looked about my size and put it in my basket. I knew nothing about measurements . . . I just assumed they would more or less do the job. But then I was cornered by a sales assistant. An older woman with a tape measure slung around her neck. She took one look at my basket and took charge of the situation.'

Phoebe was interested, despite herself.

'She measured you?'

Her mother nodded. 'I was mortified. I had never revealed

my breasts to anyone other than my reflection, in the mirror at home. To have a perfect stranger . . .' She shook her head.

Phoebe nodded in recognition. She felt a sense of calm descending.

'This woman . . . she was very matter of fact, though. She muttered something about one breast being slightly bigger than the other, but in a way that suggested this was not a surprise to her. She measured my back and then she disappeared for about ten minutes. When she came back she handed me four enormous-looking bras and told me to get dressed again.'

Phoebe stared at her mother, who turned to face her. She was smiling again.

'I was twenty-four. In the time since that picture in the south of France was taken, I had become a 34C. I must have grown three-and-a-half cup sizes in six years. I hadn't noticed. I saw myself in one way, you see. Flat chested. And that was that.

Phoebe felt herself flopping. As though her whole body was easing off on itself.

'So,' her mother said, stroking Phoebe's hair away from her face. 'What I'm trying to tell you, Phoebe – you impatient girl – is that your body does change. Sometimes in ways you don't like very much, but sometimes . . . in a way that is a pleasant surprise.'

Phoebe was silent. She felt suddenly foolish. But, relieved, of course.

'OK,' she said gruffly. 'Perhaps I will wait on that breast enlargement.'

'Good.' Her mother's eyes remained on her for a moment, before she lifted her gaze to the clock on the kitchen wall.

'Good Lord, is that the time,' she said, a little agitated. 'I completely forgot about my appointment with Doctor Seberg at six.'

She got up quickly, picking up her handbag and throwing in her car keys. 'I shouldn't be too long. It normally only takes twenty minutes. I'll make dinner when I get home.'

'Who's Doctor Seberg?' said Phoebe, already thinking about phoning Anna and spending an evening watching DVDs instead of studying.

Her mother was wrestling with her coat and moving out into the hall.

'My little magician,' she called in a comical tone, opening the front door. 'Non-invasive cosmetic procedures are his speciality . . .' But her voice was swallowed up by the sounds of the outside world.

Phoebe took a moment to register her mother's parting words, before the front door slammed, leaving the house in silence.

Except for the ticking clock on the wall.

CAITLIN MORAN

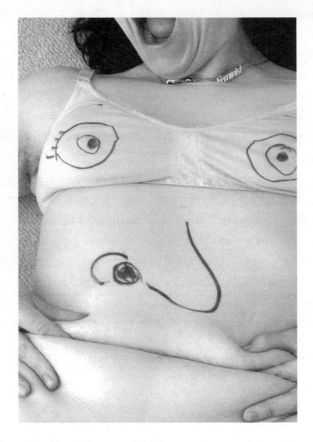

Perfectly normal to draw a face on your belly, then get your daughter to stand on a chair and take your picture. Perfectly normal.

Mooby Trap

PATRICK NESS

Though there were, obviously, two of them and each had clearly defined voices – one deeper and harsher, the other lighter and more sneering – Stewart's breasts tended to speak to him as a collective 'we'.

'We wouldn't do that if we were you,' they'd say, usually when he was about to raise his hand in class or make a joke amongst the small group he hoped were his friends or when he was looking to try a tackle on Andy Jackson during a phys ed football game. 'Too fat,' they'd say. 'No one wants to hear from/laugh with/watch the fat boy run.'

'I'm not fat,' Stewart would say to them.

'Well, we all know *that's* a lie,' they'd say, sniggering. 'We're hardly two bags of muscle, now are we?'

And Stewart would have to silently agree with them, which was unfortunate, because they could hear that, too.

'Fat, fat, fatty fat,' they'd sing. In the shower at home. In the changing room at school. Under the shirts that had seemed to fit up until the moment his breasts started talking. Under the loose jerseys and coats Stewart wore almost exclusively now.

'Boob boobity boob boob, boob boob.'

No one else seemed able to hear them, but somehow that didn't make it any better.

It had all started over the summer. Stewart's family had gone to Majorca to visit his nan and her third husband Archie. They did this every second year, and though Spain might have seemed objectively preferable to the odd-year summer trips they made to tropical Yorkshire to see his mum's family, in reality it was fifteen days of his nan drinking too many cocktails, Archie repeatedly slapping Stewart's inevitable sunburn, and Stewart's mum sighing so often a waiter once offered her his asthma inhaler.

'Getting to be quite a big boy,' his nan had said as Stewart slipped off his T-shirt for a dip in the sea.

'Oughta cut down on the chips,' Archie said, rubbing oil onto Stewart's nan's back. Sitting next to each other on their loungers, their skins were so loose and sun-browned they looked like two melted otters.

'I've got a bikini top you can borrow,' his nan chortled into her fruity cocktail.

'Mum, that's enough,' Stewart's father said from where he was blowing up waterwings for Stewart's completely accidental/'delightful surprise' of a three-year-old brother Ned, who in his toddler purview had taken to the island like a dazed native.

'They're bigger than yours, Ev,' Archie laughed, nodding at Stewart's chest.

'I said, that's *enough*,' his dad snapped.

Stewart's nan and Archie both made *oooo*ing sounds and retreated to their drinks, though not before she said, 'Like father, like son,' beneath her breath. Stewart glanced at his shirtless dad. A bit chunky, just like Stewart.

Moobs, just like Stewart.

Oh, my God, Stewart thought. *I look like* that?

'Who did you *think* we looked like?' his breasts had said, speaking up for the first time. 'Cristiano Ronaldo?'

From her own sun lounger, Stewart's mother must have seen the look of horror on her son's face, because she said, 'Don't listen to them, Stew.'

For one awful moment, Stewart thought she meant his breasts.

'Why don't you take Ned down to the water, sweetheart?' she said, kindly. 'How would you like that, Neddy?'

'*Bueno*,' Ned said, dreamily. He slipped his hand into Stewart's and as their dad headed off to the cabana bar to take a very, very long time getting everyone refills and as Stewart's mum sighed and planted her earphones in so deep they were probably touching her brain and as Nan and Archie started sharing outrage about the idiocy of a friend of theirs no one here had ever met, Stewart walked his little brother down to the water, feeling like every other tanned face on the beach was watching his breasts bounce away in the sunshine.

'They *are* watching us,' his breasts said. 'Every eyeball here.'

Stewart's skin turned a steady bright red, and it wasn't all sunburn.

149

They named themselves. Colin and Barclay. Stewart never knew where the names had come from or, for that matter, which was Colin and which was Barclay; though really, what could it possibly have mattered? He would stare at them in the mirror, hating them, hating the way they sagged there, hating how ugly they were, hating the way they poked against his school uniform, no matter which way he wore it.

He really wasn't even all that fat.

'Yeah,' they said, 'you keep telling yourself that.'

He really wasn't even all that fat. Just sort of . . . big. If he'd been more coordinated, he could have been a plausible rugby player, if his school ever played rugby, which it most certainly did not. But there were definitely other guys in his year who were fatter than him.

'They wear it differently,' his breasts said. 'More compactly, more rounded. They look like bouncers. You look like a big fat baby.'

'Shut up,' he said.

'A big fat baby *girl*,' they sneered. 'Amazing that what's so nice on a girl is so *hideous* on a boy.'

Perhaps unsurprisingly, they were particularly bad when he was in class. Week after week after week.

'Who wants to read Romeo?' Mr Duffy asked.

'We do! We do!' shouted Stewart's breasts as he sunk down into his seat, crossing his arms against them. Muffled, they still shouted. 'Two Romeos right here!'

'How about you, Stewart?' Mr Duffy said, and Stewart had a flash of terror so clear, he coughed, which Mr Duffy took as a yes. 'Grand,' he said, setting the text on Stewart's desk. There was some muffled laughter at this. Stewart glanced up towards Juliet, already standing at the front of the class. Niamh Connelly, beautiful, tall, now looking anywhere in the room except in Stewart's direction.

'You got bigger ones than *her* anyway,' his breasts said.

'Shut *up*,' Stewart hissed under his breath.

'I beg your pardon,' Mr Duffy said, suddenly stern. 'Up at the front, Stewart. Now.'

'Everyone's looking!' his breasts wailed as Stewart dragged his way to the front of the class. 'They're looking at us! Hey, everyone!'

Stewart's face went red.

'I think Stewart might be unwell, Mr Duffy,' Andy Jackson said from a desk as Stewart passed. 'He's got some horrible rash all over his head.'

'One more word, Andy,' Mr Duffy warned.

Why does being defended always make me go even redder? Stewart thought as he reached the front. He kept his eyes firmly on the text in his hand.

'They're all laughing,' his breasts said.

'Or getting ready to laugh,' one of them added, in a rare solo moment.

'This is going to be horrible!' they said, together again, gleefully.

'In your own time, Stewart,' Mr Duffy said.

Stewart felt himself go even hotter, sweat dripping down the middle of his chest, making his shirt stick to his breasts. 'Like a sauna in here!' they said.

'*Romeo, Romeo,*' Stewart mumbled, '*wherefore art thou, Romeo?*'

The laugh from the class, both so expected but also somehow surprising, made him look up. Andy Jackson was laughing openly, and everyone else seemed to be smirking, except for Sylvie Weeks, with her flaming red hair and face full of freckles, who sat in the desk just in front of Stewart, head down, apparently concentrating on her book so hard Stewart wondered for a moment if she was trying to light it on fire with her mind.

'Try again,' Mr Duffy said.

Stewart didn't know what was going on. He looked over to Niamh, who was still staring furiously away from him, but now with a foot-tapping sense of the injustice she was being put through. He looked at the text again, the words dancing across the page like ants from a kicked nest.

'*Romeo, Romeo,*' he read, '*wherefore art thou –*'

He stopped, realising his error, as the laughing of the class grew again.

'That's *my* line,' Niamh breathed to him, angrily, too late to be of any help.

His breasts were tittering uncontrollably. 'Curtain call for fat Juliet!' they crowed. 'Hey! We could play the balcony!'

'Niamh starts,' Mr Duffy said, also too late. 'You're a few lines down, Stewart.'

'Aw, Mr Duffy,' Andy Jackson said, 'he's clearly meant to be Juliet. He's a right busty wench, isn't he?'

'Yellow card, Andy,' Mr Duffy said, imposing the second highest classroom penalty on him.

But for a third time, too late to be of any use.

* * *

Stewart lay in bed, trying to calculate what kind of job he could get and how long minimum wage would take to add up to liposuction.

'Just eat less!' his breasts berated him. 'Do some exercise!'

'Hey!' Colin or Barclay said to Barclay or Colin. 'You trying to do us out of a job?'

'It's never going to happen,' the other one said, 'it never does.'

'I could just cut you off myself,' Stewart said.

'*Never going to happen*,' the breasts said again. 'You're way too big of a baby.'

They're probably right, Stewart thought, and his breasts agreed noisily.

'You're ugly,' they said.

'You're fat,' they said.

'No one will ever want you,' they said.

'You're right,' Stewart said. 'You're right, you're right, you're right, you're right, you're right.'

'Well, there's no need to *cry* about it,' his breasts said.

The next day – and probably for eternity – he became Juliet the Busty Wench at school. Sometimes just the Busty Wench, sometimes just Juliet, but it all added up to the same thing.

'Shut up,' he'd mutter, not sure if he was talking to the person who'd called him the name or to his breasts for the delight they took in it.

'Romeo, Romeo,' they'd shout to each other in a faux girly voice, 'wherefore art thou, Romeo?'

'Hey, Juliet,' Andy Jackson called to him from down the hall on his way to English class. 'Think fast!'

153

He threw something. Instinctively, Stewart put his hand up to catch it, exactly one second before he realised what it was.

Too late, he was already holding it.

'I thought maybe a C cup,' Andy said, fake sincerely, as the boys around him laughed and laughed.

'Outrage!' Stewart's breasts screamed. 'We're at least a D!'

Stewart said nothing, just flung the bra from himself as if it had caught fire. He turned his back on the laughter that was disappearing into the classroom. He faced the wall, his skin burning red, his fists pulled so tight he was in danger of cutting his palms with his fingernails.

'Dude,' his breasts said, a little warily, 'calm down. Can't you take a joke?'

Stewart raised his hands as if to strike them, as if to beat his chest flat, no matter how much it would hurt, no matter how impossible it was.

'Steady on there, Stew,' his breasts said.

'Shut up,' he hissed. 'Shut up, shut up, SHUT UP!'

He glanced around fast, suddenly aware of how loud he'd spoken.

But the hallway was empty. Class had started. Everyone had gone in except him. He was alone.

With himself.

English class awaited. More reading probably. More being ignored by Niamh. More *not* being ignored by Andy Jackson. More obliviousness from Mr Duffy.

'Hey,' his breasts said. 'Where are you going?'

Because he was already walking down the hallway in the opposite direction.

* * *

There was a large, circular building out on the grounds that the school insisted on calling 'the cricket pavilion', despite no one having played cricket there in any recent century. Full of alcoves and shaded on one side by trees, it was a truant's dream, but it was also a Grade II listed building: the school couldn't do anything about it except occasionally make sweeps for the sixth formers who went there to smoke. Stewart rushed towards it, out of breath faster than he'd like to have been ('You're hardly Mo Farah,' his breasts chuckled), and moved behind it, out of sight of the main school buildings, sitting down on one of the benches in the alcoves. He placed himself so he could avoid being seen by both the staff from the main office window and the groundsmen currently repainting the football pitch stripes.

It was only a matter of time, though; he'd certainly be caught, but for the moment, at least it wasn't English class.

'We'll still be with you when you go back in, you know,' his breasts said. 'There's no way out.'

'You tell lies,' Stewart said to them.

'Lies you believe,' they said, 'which is kind of all we need, eh?'

'Shut up,' he said. 'Just shut up.'

To his surprise, for a moment, they did. He sighed like his mum on holiday and looked out across the green. He thought of going home, but that would mean having to give his dad a reason, as it was his day to work at home and watch Neddy. He could claim stomach illness, he thought, and there were worse ways to spend a day than watching cartoons with –

'Shut up,' he heard.

'I didn't *say* anything,' he said down to his chest.

'Neither did we,' his breasts said.

But he heard it again. 'Shut up.' He stood, almost involuntarily. 'Shut up, shut up, shut up.'

There, to his left. He crept to the edge of the little alcove and looked around.

Sylvie Weeks was sitting on the next bench over.

'Shut up,' she said.

'Sorry,' Stewart said. Her head snapped up, her eyes wet with furious tears. 'I didn't think there was anyone else here.'

He couldn't quite read the confused expression on her face, as if she was uncertain for a moment what she was seeing as she looked at him.

Stewart said, 'I didn't mean to bother –'

'He's staring at us,' a nasty voice said. 'Can't even look at your face. Just looking at us, all over your body.'

Stewart blinked in surprise. 'Huh?'

Sylvie's eyes grew even wider, a different kind of shock taking over her expression.

'This girl simple-minded or something?' Stewart's breasts said. 'She'd still never agree to go out with you . . .'

They trailed off because Sylvie was staring at Stewart's chest. He instinctively put up a hand and pulled his uniform jacket shut.

'You can hear that?!' both he and Sylvie said at exactly the same time.

'She can hear us!' his breasts said, delighted. 'She's staring right at us!'

'He's staring right at us!' the other voice said, and Stewart saw Sylvie put her hand up to her neck.

'What's going on?' Stewart said.

Sylvie just shook her head in disbelief. 'But you don't even *have* freckles,' she said.

'Freckles?' Stewart asked.

'*Freckles?!*' his breasts said. 'No, lass, he's got two great big cow udders under here.'

Stewart winced, but Sylvie's face changed. She just said, 'Oh,' in a way that seemed to grasp something Stewart was missing. 'Oh.'

'Oh, what?' he asked.

She sighed and wiped her eyes dry, gathering herself with a kind of vulnerable primness. 'If I were to ask you,' she said, 'what part of yourself you hated the most . . .?'

Stewart just looked at her for a moment, then his shoulders slumped as he understood, too. 'Oh,' he said.

'Yeah,' she said, sadly.

'But what's wrong with your freckles?' Stewart said.

He heard an outbreak of uproarious laughter from the other voice, and Sylvie blushed. Stewart blushed, too, on her behalf. 'At least you're not fat,' he rushed out with.

'Fat?' she said, surprised. 'You're not fat. You're just . . . *big*.'

'*Fat*,' his breasts said. 'That's what she means by big.'

'Only a fat boy would say there's nothing wrong with us,' her freckles said.

'Shut *up*,' Sylvie said, closing her eyes in embarrassment.

Stewart felt like he should probably leave, that that's what she probably wanted, privacy, a place to suffer this humiliation alone, just like he had . . .

But maybe not.

He was surprised a little to find himself sitting down next to her, his hand still holding his uniform jacket shut, not that it had made much difference up to now. Sylvie opened her eyes, but didn't say anything.

She didn't ask him to leave, though.

'I thought it was just me,' he finally said.

'Everybody's got *something*,' Sylvie said.

'Do you think that's true?'

She looked angry for a moment. 'It had *better* be.'

They sat in silence. Then Stewart realised it actually *was* silence. Sylvie glanced over at him. She'd noticed it, too.

'It won't last,' she whispered, though there was a clear hope in it that she was wrong. 'They'll start back up again.'

'Probably,' he whispered back.

But it lingered, the silence, and they sat, still, afraid that moving might break it.

Eventually, after what seemed like hours, but what was probably only a few minutes – though everyone knows a few minutes is all it ever takes for the world to spin just a little differently – he said, almost to himself, 'You know, I've always really liked freckles.'

Which was all it took to set everything talking again.

But . . .

His eyes met hers as the voices berated away, and as she realised it, too, she gave him a surprised smile.

He found himself giving one back.

Did his breasts ever shut up as he grew older and kept meaning to eat more vegetables and do more exercise? No. Did her freckles, no matter how many layers of sunscreen she applied in an attempt at melanin birth control? Nope, not for the entire rest of the life they were both quietly astonished to find themselves spending with each other.

But when they were together, her hand in his, and they were looking into each other's eyes again, and the sometimes loud, sometimes ugly noise of the world surrounded them, well, then, at those moments, who could possibly have been interested in listening?

Upfront

ERIN O'CONNOR

The first time I became aware of my boobs was when I went walking with my friend's parents. I was horrified aged eight when my friend Lorraine stripped to the waist and marched through the park with utter indifference to my mortification. As a later indication of my prudishness, I struck up a painful pros and cons conversation with her mum and dad about why I should leave my top on. They were amused and exasperated all at once – I was adamant that my *très bien* T-shirt would remain faithfully in place and relieved that my moral alignment had once again been restored.

It's not that I wasn't familiar with boobs. As a small Catholic child I saw Jesus's boobs every day and sometimes my mother's, admittedly when her cleverly concealing face cloth slipped during bath time. Thankfully they weren't hairy like my dad's, but sort of eager and buoyant with a will of their own – prompting both accelerated fear and excitement in equal measure. Ours was a prominently female household and growing up with Mum and my two sisters meant that tits and bits were unavoidable (I sigh on behalf of Dad). I remember my big sis Kel getting her first job on the underwear stall at the local indoor market and eyeballing (albeit lids half cast) the exotic paraphernalia she brought home at discount price. I didn't waste any time trying it all on in her absence. Claire, my fellow conspirator and youngest sister, once mistook a pair of crotchless pants as a bra, with the open crotch comfortably slipping over her petit head as her arms flapped about trying to find an outlet either side. As quickly as her naivety had betrayed her, she literally sprung one spring, leaving me and my inverted nipples firmly behind.

As my first day of secondary school approached, I bought myself a new alice band to coordinate with my new uniform and a set of new vests – yes, you heard me correctly. Upon reaching that momentous day I learned quickly that boobs were tits and tits meant only one thing – bras! The protruding bow that hung over my blouse served only to expose my still child-like body, and having received what can only be described as a wedgie of the upper carriage from a boy in the fourth year, I was sent into a blind frigid panic. You could call it a life-changing day, not least because it was to be another seven years before I went bra-less again. Not one, you understand, but two, worn one on top of the other, padded and intricately scaffolded to give the illusion of normality and inclusiveness. The indescribable physical discomfort I felt was akin to wearing a toddler's harness with egg boxes attached – but to endure the pain of going without would have been a far greater punishment within my adolescent mind.

As Mother Nature would have it, I had to wait until my sweet sixteenth before puberty lazily stirred within. The fact that the one (OK, two) things I had wanted so desperately to arrive hadn't, was in itself a reason for martyrdom. On top of it, I had a shnozz that apparently knew no bounds, protruding from my face to give me an air of haughty assertion that betrayed the still shy girl within. My respite came in the form of ballet, where boobs weren't needed but body strength and determination were. My 183 cm body began gradually to unfold itself, and for the first time I felt good about my tits as they clung safely, nestled within the pre-moulded bosom of my spandex leotard. Alert, pert, proud and nipply – yes nipply! My body was responsive – or perhaps I was beginning to respond to it. Oh how malleable and 'on demand' they were. I began to tweak and play with them at regular intervals – they were having a regular coming-out party of their own and continue to be upstanding!

To cut a long story short, my boobs have proved to be a source of enormous discussion over the years. It's true to say that as a teenager I thought about getting 'them done', but thank God I was broke as it meant that I sat quite literally with the problem. I remember early on in my modelling career, a hairdresser in LA advised me to get my nose reduced and to expand my bosoms. Now, I'm NOT infallible to my own self-criticism; however, something wonderful happened in response. I realised I had punished my lovely, hard-working, healthy body for years with feelings of inadequacy and 'not quite right' syndrome – how dare someone else tell me what's wrong with me!? In that moment my stubbornness took over and with almighty gusto I told the bozo in question to do one. He was aghast and ignorant to my new-found conviction and I began to protect my body, just as it was, with all my might.

In general both men and women have intervened, offering me constant solutions to my body issues – not mine, theirs – because it seems that even if I accept my body it doesn't necessarily mean other people do. Some ask, with genuine concern, if I will be 'relieved to get a boob job once my modelling career is over'? I am always astonished by this question because to me it brings into question my womanhood, as if by not fixing the problem I am somehow incomplete. I can assure you that I am all woman, in attitude as well as physical attribute. I revel in my femininity so how could I betray that by succumbing to a social stigma of what's considered right and wrong, socially acceptable, even? I have collected a couple of amusing anecdotes over the years to satisfy the reader's appetite: How will you breastfeed? Did you have them removed? It's a humbling thing to put aside someone else's ignorance in order to stay sane. One journalist, a woman, splashed my tits over a double-paged spread in a tabloid newspaper, seemingly indignant that I had chosen to wear a revealing dress. Her response? Contrived references such as 'part-time ironing board', etc. My point is, SHE wasn't comfortable with my body, therefore I was punished and subjected to public humiliation.

As a prerequisite to accepting my body/boobs just as they are, it has given me enormous empathy and respect for all other women. Our boobs are precious, gentle and sensitive but also proud, happy and upstanding in a very powerful, responsive way. I'm all for variety in tit/tittage of all different

163

shapes and sizes – heck I have fondled my sisters' (of blood and friend variety) enough over the years, and they mine in equal appreciation!

Garnering both positive and negative descriptions of my body over the years has, at times left me feeling very uncomfortable – I have worked hard to be kind to myself and quit judging. After all, my tits have served me well – they work, they satisfy and I am eternally grateful to be healthy. Why shouldn't I be upfront about them?

PS I haven't worn a bra in 15 years!

SCRIPT TITLE

Written by

Name of First Writer

Based on, If Any

Address
Phone Number

PILLOW TALK, BY CHRIS O'DOWD.

INT. TEENAGE GIRL'S BEDROOM – NIGHT

A girl, 16, lies in bed.
A cheeky boy has just climbed out the window.
Under the covers –

LISA

I'm fine, I'm fine, I don't want to talk about
it.

REGINA

OK. It's just . . . you don't seem fine. You
seem a little tender.

LISA

What the hell is so wrong with me?

REGINA

Nothing, you're beautiful, you are –

LISA

Bullshit! Bullshit, Regina. Night after
night I just lie here, freezin' my tip off
like a lonely shadow, while you cavort over
there like the feckin' Queen of Sheeba.

REGINA
You're being very sensitive . . .

LISA
Of course I'm sensitive, and he knows
exactly why, and it's the same reason he's
being so top-half friendly this week.

REGINA
Well, fanny's house guest has been no picnic
either.

LISA
Stupid, stupid, stupid boys. They always
ignore the introverted one –

REGINA
(under her breath)
– inverted –

LISA
What was that?

REGINA
Eh . . . nothing . . . I was just agreeing
with you.

                    LISA
Does he think I'm sick? They're stretch
   marks, not leprosy, you knob!

                  REGINA
What you need to remember is . . . Jimmy is
               left handed.

                    LISA
Well, ambidextrous Andy did the same
nonsense. Titism is all it is, plain and
                  simple.

                  REGINA
You're not plain and simple, Lisa –

                    LISA
Easy for you to say, old piercy Pip over
there, steering palms like a big silver hand
                magnet . . .

                  REGINA
Hey! You didn't have to deal with the
               infection.

                    LISA
I know, I'm sorry. It's not your fault. I'm
            sorry, I'm just . . .

                    REGINA
         Hey, she should guide them more.

                     LISA
       Like it's not enough she puts us on show at
           parties, and then during the day -

Silence.

                    REGINA
         No support at all, I know, I do.

                     LISA
     Another 15 years of this shit and then she'll
         just turn us into big food troughs.

                    REGINA
         Hey, at least we're in it together.

                     LISA
     Yeah. I love you R - wait, what's this . . .
     No, no, don't turn over, sleep on your back
                    ya bit—

                                   The End.

My Date with Destiny . . .
in the Form of Boobies

DERMOT O'LEARY

I've never been much of a boobies man (OK, from here on in, can we call them breasts? Otherwise we could be in a second-year common room looking at *Fiesta* magazine in the 80s and trust me, this could be a very dark place).

When my friends were all hunkered down, transfixed by the screen, trying in vain to get dealt a straight flush to beat 'Sam Fox's strip poker' on the ZX Spectrum, circa 1987, I was wondering, firstly, how do you know the rules of poker aged fourteen? (They didn't.) And secondly, there's no way the lovely Sam is going to give up a brief glance at her heavily pixelated crown jewels to a group of adolescents who can't play poker for toffee (she didn't).

Don't get me wrong, I adore – did you hear me? – ADORE the female form, in all its forms! It's just that when it comes to breasts, it's much like your taste in chicken; you're a breast guy or a leg guy. And when you were a fourteen-year-old boy you DID NOT say you were a leg man, we had them too, as well as bums, it just didn't add up, it was the equivalent of not having red blood cells coursing through your veins.

So now, twenty-five years later, it gives me great pleasure to say I've seen the error of my ways, and I realise that being attentive to one's breasts is of paramount importance to women (and men) of all ages.

My wake-up call came at The Pride of Britain Awards a couple of years ago. I was giving an award, and it's always been the most worthy, thought-provoking 'put your own stupid problems into context' kind of night. Think toddlers with super-human strength pulling their grannies out of burning buildings, or OAPs walking on their hands for charity from Lands End to John O'Groats . . . If you're not in floods of tears within ten minutes, then you're made of stone. It quite simply restores your faith in your fellow man.

I wasn't on the table I expected to be on, but I was with friends, so I didn't make a fuss and sat where I was put. One hour in, a blonde, bald bombshell and her twin sister bowled up to my table. Kris and Maren were friendly, but were certainly on a mission.

'And why have you changed your seat? You're supposed to be sat with us.'

This was bad. A: I had no real idea what they were talking about, and B: A cancer patient was telling me off . . . which is not a good look, especially when you don't know why.

I obviously folded like my fourteen-year-old friends' poker hands, and sat them down for a chat, and chat we did, all night. I was vaguely aware of the issues around breast cancer, but

Kris and her sister Maren's knowledge combined with their passion and energy was a much-needed education.

Two years (and two half-marathons) down the line, I'm proud to be a patron of one of the hardest-working and dynamic charities I've ever worked with. The girls at CoppaFeel! and their merry band of game disciples (who incidentally also bake a mean cake) travel the country to universities and festivals spreading awareness and the word of all things booby (curses, I've said it again) to both women and men. Hell, they're so on it, they now even stage their own festival! ('Festifeel' . . . very strong) to spread the good word.

And much like my experience with them, others have found . . . they are pretty hard to say no to.

Turns out I am a boob man after all.

DAWN O'PORTER

A few years ago a friend of mine went for a mammogram and she was so scared of what they might find that she fainted whilst still clamped into the machine. If you have ever had a mammogram you will know how hard they squeeze your boobs, so you will know how likely it is that if you faint, you will have to, um . . . hang? Awful as this is, it's also quite funny. I thought maybe poetry was the best way to tackle it.

The Booby Trap

It's an awkward moment in a woman's life,
When the fear of going under the knife
Losing your hair
Losing your life,
Means you can barely stand on your shivering limbs
As you imagine your loved ones singing hymns.

You flop your breast onto a cold metal plate
And wait for the machine to decide your fate.
It squeezes so hard

It makes you cry
How will you ever say goodbye?
Forced into an unnatural slump
You obsess about them finding a lump.

As the robot gropes you
All of those hopes you
Have of growing old and wise
Vanish in the vision of your own demise.
The worries of what this result could mean
Overflow your brain
Wipe it clean.
No air can find its way to your head
One word is on your lips
Dead
Dead
Dead.

Stop being so silly, you make yourself think
But further away your faculties sink.
As the machine takes pictures
Snap
Snap
Snap
You're left hanging
By the tit
From the Booby Trap.

Beauty and the B(r)easts

HOLLY BAXTER – THE VAGENDA

Once upon a time, my mother thought her giant breasts were 32As. I was a knock-kneed thirteen-year-old, and I needed a clean bra from the laundry when she told me to just borrow one of hers. 'We're the same size, after all,' she said, jiggling her giant bazookas next to my tiny teenage pimples. Something had clearly gone awry.

Mum's sense of dimensions had been drastically altered by years of her older sister – a woman endowed with chesticles so huge that they began to eventually curve her spine, whispering to her, Gollum-like, in the bedroom they shared, that 'dental floss with knots in it would do as a bra for you'. During her delicate formative years, Mother had been subjected to regular taunts about fried eggs on ironing boards while sitting down for lunch, and offered membership to the ltty Bitty Titty Brigade when she came in for dinner. By middle age, she'd become practically apologetic whenever anybody set eyes on her perfectly shapely frame. She considered her breasts a personal failure. It all came to a head that Tuesday when the laundry was late out of the dryer. Such was the success of her sister's teasing, it turned out, that my poor mum had been squashing herself into teenage training bras for forty years, well after giving birth to two children and breastfeeding them to boot. Most people knew Auntie Susan as a formidable character, but nobody had quite realised the true extent of her powers until I peered into my mother's underwear drawer. Amongst the Spanx, stockings, and seamless knickers was a terrifying truth in the form of a neatly folded row of A-cup brassieres. Their strained straps and misshapen holders spoke of decades of knocker oppression.

Something had to be done, and the solution came to me in a cold sweat a few nights later, as I lay contemplating the effects of squashing pumpkins into salt shakers. The only person with the courage and ability to tackle such a chronic case of funbag dysmorphia was the stern lady in the changing rooms at Marks & Spencer. Armed only with a measuring tape, she would surely set to work in dismantling Mum's problems with proportion. An objective instrument of measurement would finally afford her the proof of her own body, and any doubts would be quelled by the measurer's strident sense of purpose. The plan was watertight – tighter, indeed, than a 32A on a glamour model.

A few weeks later, we put the plan into action and slayed the beast of self delusion. Mum was officially declared a 34DD, to much aplomb, and picked out bras in her actual bra size for the first time in her life. Freed from the shackles of her previously undersized underwear, which had been leaving red welts along her sides for as long as she could remember, she finally saw her body for what it really was. Clothes fitted in ways that they had never fitted before; her revolutionised underwear drawer was a joy to behold. The spell had been broken.

As for me, well, I learnt from previous generations' mistakes and got myself a measuring tape once I'd grown a pair. I live in blissful harmony with all of my bras, which live happily ever after, pressed against my chest. And I definitely can't borrow my mother's underwear anymore, which is really a great relief for all of us.

Like all good fairy tales, of course, this one wouldn't be complete without a didactic conclusion. And so the moral of this story is that everyone can get silly about boobs, but it's worth not being too silly about your own.

Boob Envy

RHIANNON LUCY COSSLETT – THE VAGENDA

I didn't really pay much attention to my breasts until I realised that they weren't growing at the same rate as everyone else's. While girls in my class began to develop ample bosoms at the tender age of eleven, I remained 'flat as a pancake' for most of my teenage years. I came of age in the laddish decade that was the nineties; when humungous fake tits started to dominate the wipe-clean pages of *Loaded* and almost filled page three of the *Sun*, which was stuffed quickly and covertly down the backs of school radiators by the boys, in its entirety. Meanwhile, Geri Halliwell, my idol, had a cleavage that I could only dream about, and my friend has hilariously nicknamed hers 'Pinky and Perky'.

It was around this time that I began to get the message loud and clear: that the breasts maketh the woman, and that, as such, I was still very much a girl. The boys would ping the girls' bra straps outside French, and laugh when they sensed no lump of elastic underneath my polyester polo shirt. A strange kind of hierarchy emerged in the corridors between classes; the girls with the bras were, of course, on top. Having a bra became a status symbol — it was, after all, the decade of the Wonderbra — and eventually I demanded one not out of necessity, but as a result of peer pressure.

I longed for the smushed together, pneumatic 'boobs' (they were always boobs, not breasts) of the girls on telly, and would cry into my mother's much more ample pair on more than one occasion. Magazines didn't help, either. I was aware from a very young age (too young, I'd argue) that I wasn't quite up to scratch compared with, say, Melinda Messenger, and that these women embodied a kind of cheeky, plasticky sexuality that wasn't really me at all. At the same time, the existence of the lads' mags gave me the uncomfortable feeling that having tits automatically made a certain kind of man feel that he could make you the subject of scrutiny. When a friend of mine complained that a pervy old geezer had leered at her bosom before telling her to 'put them away, love', I felt a bit sick. Some of the girls at school had much older boyfriends, as though their breasts had made them women inside as well as out. One of them showed me her lovebite in the toilets, small and lurid and red, right next to her nipple. I didn't envy her.

In my mid-teens, I became a goth, for a bit at least, and discovered eyeliner and boys. The realisation that the young lad with his hand up your top is too busy counting his lucky stars to question you about your cup size can be a powerful one. In my experience, you worry more about 'the girls' before you're having sex than you ever do once you're doing it. Provided that they're healthy, of course. 'Just wait till you get pregnant', my mum would say, whenever I moaned about my chest. I didn't fancy that much, ta (I still don't) and plus, I liked the effect the pill had on their size.

Then, aged eighteen, I moved to Paris, and miraculously stopped caring. Whether it was the string of boyfriends that followed or the fact that the French in general seem less obsessed with all things boob-related than the English, perhaps because the women there are smaller and more gamine (if they had the comedy boobs of the tabloids they'd be constantly falling flat on their faces – *ce n'est pas très cool*). Either way, my breasts just became another part of me – nothing to worry about at all, and perfectly sized when it came to encasing them in gossamer-thin scraps of lacy French lingerie. Granted, they're smaller than the average pair, but as the years have gone by I've learned to love them. I doubt somehow that they'll ever make their way downwards to my waist, but I'd like to see them try.

VICTORIA WHITE

My mum has boobs. Nice squashy ones that sort of fall out of her bra when she takes it off. When boys were mean to me as a teenager or ditched me for Kirsty Grantham in the year above me because she let them touch her breasts, my mum would cuddle me into her squashy boobs and let me cry there. Growing up I assumed I'd have boobs like my mum – as my dad doesn't have them it's hard to imagine what his side of the gene pool has by way of boobs! But as eleven, twelve, thirteen passed and I still had no reason to go to that bit in Marks & Spencer where they sell early-years bras, it became clear that Dad boobs I had – literally. I am now forty and I still have no boobs. And strangely, as I have every other body hang-up known to woman, I am fine with this. I like that I can wear really low-cut tops and not look slutty. I like that even on a 'fat' day I know I can wear black trousers and from the waist up look sort of skinny. I like that I can buy those meshy Calvin Klein sports bras that offer no support whatsoever and are really just two triangles of fabric held together by string. Best of all, I know, for certain, that my breasts will never hang over my belt like the dinner ladies' at school used to. But I sort of feel sad that my sons will never be squished to my breasts in a maternal way. When they get dumped my only way of consoling them will be with reassuring words, like, 'Don't worry, wanna go Nandos?'

LAURA WHITMORE

I always wanted boobs. I think I may have lit a candle for them as a kid after mass praying. . . Although I'm sure I told my mother I was praying for world peace.

At age thirteen, I was still wearing one of those cotton vest tops (the type your five-year-old brother wears) and I remember changing after a swimming lesson and seeing that one of my classmates had an ACTUAL bra! I'll never forget the look she gave me as she gazed at my perplexed, forlorn face staring at her and then dropped her eyes down to the baggy bobbly off-white vest that was hiding . . . Well, hiding nothing, as I didn't have anything to hide. She smirked and I died inside.

I went straight home that afternoon and bellowed through the front door, 'Mammy, I need a BRA!!!' I definitely didn't, but as Mammy Whitmore's only daughter, she conceded.

Aged sixteen and going to the local disco, I only had two small bumps where my breasts should be. I had a solution. Two padded bras. Now this may sound stupid, but I swear it was my saviour. Thankfully no guys came near me so there was no fear of anyone finding out my situation as they rummaged in the 'under jumper/over bra area'.

My friend's mam used to sow her two bras together, which seemed extreme, but even more effective. One bra slipping below the other can end up with the dreaded four breasts look, which is actually worse than the flat-chested look.

I was seventeen when my boobs properly blossomed into 32Ds. Of course they didn't grow at the same time – oh God, wouldn't that have made life so much easier. So I had to wait at least six months for the left one to catch up with the right one. We've been on an incredible journey, my boobs and I, and we still have our arguments, especially when they prevent me from fitting into a designer sample-size dress, but they're mine and I've accepted them . . . for better or for worse.

Uplifted

MATT WHYMAN

Nobody knew what to say when Eric came to work with the tits. In fact, nobody said anything for several shifts. Not to his face, at any rate. Even meeting his eyes was a struggle, what with the rack that had materialised under his shirt.

'It can't be a boob job,' I whispered on a break from the phones. 'Can it?'

I was in the canteen with Melanie and Tom from Retentions. Eric was standing in the queue with his tray, though we doubted he could see it on account of his cleavage. It was just so unexpected from such a clean-cut, regular guy.

'He's a middle-aged man, married with kids.' This was Tom, convinced it was a wind-up or a thing for charity. 'He's got some socks up there.'

'Big socks,' Mel noted. 'Massive.'

For a moment, the three of us watched as Eric took his turn in front of the lunch technician behind the sneeze counter. On seeing him, or rather his breasts, she reached for a spatula as if preparing to swat a fly. Eric greeted her, and then pointed to the sausage and mash. It took a moment for the poor woman to blink and serve him, but he didn't seem to mind. In fact, Eric looked really quite cheery as he took his tray to the table. Just then, he stood out more for his mood than the mammaries I believed he'd had fitted. Like everyone else, Eric was normally doleful and sullen. This was a call centre, after all. We came here to earn a living, and paid for it with our souls.

It was Greg from Assurance who finally asked him straight up. Eric had just walked into the gents, where the man was in mid flow. He left a urinal between them, as is convention, though Greg had no interest in seizing a glimpse of what he was packing down there.

'Mate,' he said finally, on zipping himself up. 'Are they for real?'

Eric looked around, beaming broadly.

'My bosoms?' he said to clarify, as if there was anything else of note about him, and finished with a deft shake. 'Sure.'

It must have taken Greg some guts to just ask the guy direct. Nobody else had begun to find a way to address the issue. Even so, when Eric replied so freely, it left poor Greg quite unprepared to follow it up.

'Right,' he said, and hurried across to the taps. 'Thanks.'

When Eric appeared at the sink beside his, Greg responded by washing his hands vigorously.

'It's OK,' said Eric after a moment. 'There's no reason for either of us to be embarrassed. If you have any questions, feel free to ask me anything.'

'I'm good,' said Greg, who then backed away from the sink and returned to work with soap on his hands.

Once word of the encounter spread across the centre, it wasn't long before people mustered the courage to take things further with Eric. I was on the phones when our line manager approached his booth. She lived by the company rule book. If a clause were added to cut out our tongues, she'd have been the first to find a knife and instruct us to form an orderly queue. At the time, I was having my ear chewed off by a customer with anger issues. This happened so often throughout each shift that I'd learned to tune out the ranting and listen to conversations around me. It didn't do much for my spirits, but I'd yet to take the lift to the roof terrace and jump off. I sat up straight in my seat, which allowed me to see over the edge of the divider as the woman who signed off our time sheets perched on Eric's desk and asked him to skip the next call.

'I think you know why I'm here,' she said, possibly unaware that every phone drone within earshot was now watching them closely.

Eric looked puzzled, and yet he didn't stop smiling.

'Is it my performance?' he asked.

'No, that's fine. It's your . . . enhancement.'

In the pause before she put her concern into words, I watched the colour in her cheeks begin to blossom. Eric simply sat there, with that blissful expression set across his face.

'I had them done on my week off,' he said, cupping his chest as if to show her. 'The soreness has almost gone now. I can't wear an underwire for a couple more weeks, but that hasn't stopped me shopping for bras. I'm building quite a collection!'

At first, it looked as if our line manager would respond by fainting. Instead, with what must've been a herculean effort, she mustered the focus to nod and clear her throat.

'Eric, is everything OK at home? Do we need to know about any difficulties?'

Eric looked to one side for a moment, still looking strikingly sunny, and then shook his head.

'It's all good,' he said simply, just as his phone began to ring. He gestured at the headset on his desk. 'Shall I?'

Our line manager didn't appear to register the phone for a moment. When Eric repeated himself, it seemed to come as quite a shock to her.

'Of course,' she said, and gave him space so he could take the call. 'Sorry.'

It was no understatement to say that I loathed my job. Tied up in targets, there was no room to be human. Seeking new horizons, in the current climate, was frankly a pipe dream. All we could do was hit the numbers until the time arrived when we'd all be replaced by computers. As a result, an air of utter desolation hung over the call centre cubicles.

Every now and then, the line managers would be sent in to pull a stunt in a bid to force some laughter, but it was always so fake that it teetered on tears. They'd been known to wear fairy wings or rubber rings, and once a month we'd assemble to play the kind of motivational games that made a bullet in the head seem like a kinder option. So, it was striking how Eric's spirit seemed to sky rocket following his breast augmentation. We began using the technical term after chatting to him about the procedure. As more people braved a conversation, it just seemed like less of a big deal. Eric wasn't embarking on some gender reassignment, we learned. What's more, having discussed his reasons in full with his family, he'd undergone the procedure with their blessing and support. He did admit to Les in Escalations that the idea just popped into his head one day, but he stressed that it had taken several months before he decided to make the investment. That was how Eric described it sometimes, as if he'd placed money in a savings account with a high return.

'I wish I'd done it earlier in life,' he once told me in between calls. I hadn't started the conversation. Eric had heard me quietly tapping my forehead against the desk in a bid to just feel something, and popped up looking positively beatific. I'd asked him what he had to be so buoyant about, but by then he didn't need to spell it out. In fact, now that he was free to wear any bra of his choosing, the balcony number that he favoured made him appear even more uplifted. 'I appreciate it might look unconventional,' he added, as my phone began to ring. 'But what matters most is how it makes me feel on the inside.'

Back in my bedsit that evening, after a ready meal in front of some reality TV on repeat, I turned in for an early night. I had nothing exciting to get up for, but sleep was the only time I could slip from my grim existence. I shed my work uniform, which always seemed so pointless when we were invisible to the public, and caught sight of my reflection in the mirror. Pulling back my shoulders, I considered myself for a moment. For a man in his mid-forties, my hairline was on the wane, while my waist was thickening no matter how many extra miles

I put in on the treadmill. Studying my reflection, I cupped my chest and pushed both inwards and up. Frankly, there was enough give there for me to shape them into something more becoming. I held them in place for a short while. Then, dismissing an idea that sprang into my mind, I turned to my teeth to see if I needed to floss.

Six weeks after Eric's transformation, during which time he had nailed four silver stars for his shirt pocket in recognition of his call turnover, I had a chance to feel his personal work first hand. I wasn't alone. Having walked into the gents, I found a small queue of colleagues awaiting their turn. Eric didn't seem to mind at all. He had even unbuttoned his shirt to enable a close examination. At first it looked like a sexual thing, but the guys were quick to stress this was purely driven by curiosity.

'Be my guest,' said Eric, when I caught his eye. 'Cop a feel.'

It had been some time since I'd placed my palms on bare breasts. The divorce had seen to that several years back. Tentatively, having warmed my hands by blowing on them, I covered Eric's chest with my fingers splayed.

'Wow,' I said, on noting how his nipples impressed upon my palms. 'They're really kind of perfect.'

'I know,' said Eric proudly. 'It's been the making of me.'

I made way for Will from Relations and Support, but studied Eric's face the whole time. He just seemed so jubilant to be sharing this moment with us. It was as if his enhancement wasn't something he had done for himself but the benefit of everyone around him.

'Man, that felt good,' said Will, before leading everyone back to work with what was clearly a spring in his step.

I had been in the job as long as Eric. We started in the same week, in fact. Back then, I took to the phones with vigour and vim. Now, I just felt worn out and washed up. I worked to pay the rent, the maintenance and bills, with a little tucked away each month for a rainy day. I couldn't remember the last time the sun had shone, but then nor did it truly pour. Every morning I awoke to the sound of drizzle, which was marginally more powerful than my power shower on full tilt. At work, hearing Eric in the cubicle next to mine was about the only thing that stopped me from heading home, slotting my head in the oven and then wishing that I was on gas. He laughed and joked with the callers, wishing every single one of them a nice day as his way of signing off. It should've made me grind my molars down to stumps. Instead, it sounded so heartfelt that I wished I could muster the same spirit. Even on tea breaks, when it was customary to just sit there staring at the walls, people began to gravitate towards Eric for conversation and entertainment. Any men who viewed his breasts with suspicion or ridicule were quickly won over, while I noted how the women seemed completely at ease in his company.

All I wanted to do was experience just a hint of Eric's joy for life. That winter, when I left the call centre with him one evening, and just before we went our separate ways, I turned to him and asked outright.

'Your breasts,' I said. 'Would a pair do the same thing for me?'

It was a chill evening. Even in his quilted coat, zipped up

to the throat, there was no hiding Eric's cleavage. In a way, I had grown so used to seeing his boobs that the man would've looked odd without them.

'It all comes down to making the most of what little we have,' he said eventually, before sharing something with me that I hadn't expected.

I watched him head into the night, both hands buried in his pockets and his shoulders swinging with each stride. A moment later, I found myself nodding, as if I understood Eric's reasons for what he'd just told me. It all made sense now I saw things through his eyes. Above all, men had been admiring and desiring the bosom for all the wrong reasons. We had denied ourselves the chance to look and feel *magnificent*. It was all a question of confidence, I realised. I had a life to celebrate, and not squander for a moment longer, even if that meant taking risks.

I knew where to find the clinic. It wasn't far off my route home. As I'd made the same journey twice a day for a lifetime, even the detour felt like a liberation. There would be no going back. My rainy day had arrived. I didn't even think about bailing as I approached the clinic's revolving door. If anything, I felt like I had come home. I pushed through, and found myself in a reception that was so blindingly white it might've been modelled on heaven. The lady behind the desk looked up from her monitor and asked how she could help.

'I'm interested in an enhancement,' I told her, adding, 'top half,' in case she was in any doubt.

'Then you've come to the right place,' she said, without any hesitation or surprise. 'If you'd just like to complete this assessment form first. After that we can discuss your options in more detail.'

'Great,' I said, and took the documents from her. 'I'll fill it in right now. Might as well seize the moment!'

It felt great to be fired up by something for once. I couldn't wait for this journey to begin.

'You're welcome to take a seat over there,' she said, gesturing behind me. 'If you can find a space.'

I smiled and turned, faltering only when I saw the sofa and the fact that two of the three spots had been taken. Still, there was enough room in the middle, and I felt sure the pair busy signing off their forms would squeeze up for me.

'Have you heard?' I asked, on dropping into the seat between Tom from Retentions and Les in Escalations. 'Eric is moving on.'

Storm in an AA Cup

LARA WILLIAMSON

I loved the 1939 movie of *The Wizard of* Oz. I loved it so much I could have pooped rainbows and it would have been no biggie. Dorothy was my girl crush du jour with her cutesy gingham pinafore, her silken pigtails and her feet made of rubies. I knew her songs by heart, even that funny verse about chimneys in *Over the Rainbow*. Bored in the Christmas holidays, a gang of us decided to put on a pantomime for the street we lived in. We had to make our own amusement somehow. Well, the rest is history, because in my opinion *The Wizard of* Oz was the best pantomime known to mankind and the Dorothy part was going to be mine, my pretties.

My mates didn't argue with the plan. Well, who would when faced with someone in a gingham apron and their mother's red slingbacks? During rehearsals, I spent many an hour wowing them with my impromptu whipping of my hair back and forth, running from side to side, my arms Muppet-flailing, and then falling into the hastily painted cardboard backdrop of Kansas. I was in an imaginary tornado, you see. I WAS living and breathing Dorothy Gale. My friends recognised me for the visionary genius I was.

Oh yes, I took it seriously. Street show or not, you can't channel Dorothy Gale half-heartedly. That would be criminal. For a start, the red slingbacks needed rhinestones. When I mooted the idea of gluing rubies to her shoes, my mother said no, fearing she'd have to walk the yellow brick road to town every time she wanted a bag of oven chips. Apparently, a modern-day Dorothy wasn't all about the money. Or the bling. My mother was Miss Gulch in disguise. I thought about offering her the part.

The sad sequin-less ruby slippers without rubies I could just about cope with, but finding out that Judy Garland was actually sixteen and quite curvy when she played Dorothy, not so much. All would have been fine if I wasn't still under a vest. I wanted everything to be perfect for my Dorothy homage and that meant growing my boobs in time for the performance and allowing them to spring forth like Toto frolicking in a field of poppies, or puppies. Okay, I admit it. It had ten per cent to do with Dorothy and ninety per cent because I JUST WANTED BIG BOOBS!

Give it a few weeks and you'll be juggling cantaloupes in the Emerald City, I thought. Those flying monkeys won't be able to carry you because of the weight in your front carriage. Slow to catch on to this idea, my boobs remained tiny. With the performance looming I attempted to show them their true potential by shoving tennis balls down there. A sort of: 'Hello boobs! Wake up, you lazy lumps of fat, milk glands and tissue!'

They stayed more Munchkin than melon. Never fear, there was one thing I hadn't tried: the power of mind over matter. I mind and my boobs matter. My boobs were not weak; they would rise to this challenge. Had they not already survived some eejit in the chip shop, battered sausage in one hand, honking them with the other? Had they not survived me falling off a wall and slamming the concrete with my entire body? Yes, I put my teeth through my lip but my chest was made of steel girders. Destroy my mouth but mess with my boobs at your peril, concrete pavement. Ha! And so it began. Day one: I waved my palms over my naked boobs shouting, 'A-bra-ca-boob-ra!' After fifty further attempts, I figured I was a candidate for RSI. Day two: I swore there was tingling in my boobs. Proper actual internal prickling, the kind of which only comes from one million Lilliputians wielding needle swords inside your boobs *or* swelling. I opted for swelling as I thought the Lilliputians were probably elsewhere, chaining Gulliver. Okay, I couldn't see any movement in my breast department but as my mother said, 'You don't need to see God to know he exists.'

Um . . . yeah.

Day three: I learnt ways to make my mini-mammaries mahoosive. Move forward like a juggernaut of jugs, that's what I'd do. After much research, I massaged them with butter. Hands up, who'd like to smell of eau de croissant in their quest for big boobs? Me, that's who. Hands up, who'd like to eat dry toast because there's no butter left? Excellent! Day four: the tape measure was out. They had grown a millionth of a millimetre. That's cool, right? One million of anything is awesome. Except germs. Today, a millionth of a millimetre: tomorrow, straight to

Dollywood on the fast bus out of Flatsville. Day five: Glinda the Good. I'm not ashamed to admit, I prayed to the good witch. 'Wave your wand and give me some boobs or else,' I said. I was good with threats. Unfortunately, no kaleidoscope bubble floated into my bedroom. I swiftly followed this with: 'I'll die if you don't make me a C cup and then you'll be sorry.' I pondered that this threat was a touch tricky as it involved actual dying. On day six and seven I drank loads of milk and ate carbs. Before long, I was so full the gingham apron barely stretched across my middle. Time to stop, I thought, before I ended up in the wrong production. Two words: Augustus Gloop.

Three days before the big Dorothy moment, I sprained my ankle on dog poop. All I can say is using a hedge to wipe dog dirt off your rollerskated foot while balancing on the other rollerskated foot is the highway to an elephantine ankle. But the show goes on and my street performance as Dorothy went ahead, despite the agony. There was a standing ovation, no less. Perhaps it was pity applause for my perky little peanuts caught up in a Beaufort number twelve. Or maybe it was because the Munchkins got distracted and sat on their mothers' laps. Or was it sympathy that I had to hobble down the yellow-bed-sheet-cum-brick-road, leaning on a scarecrow who when he shouted that he needed a brain an audience member (from the house at the end of the street) hollered back, 'You think you've got problems, mate? Dorothy needs a new leg!' Who knows? Who cares? My ankle was leaden but the feather lightness of my boobs was liberating. I didn't have to worry about my baps popping out of the apron. Nor did I think for one second that they'd zoom over my shoulder like calamine-lotion-coloured ear muffs. I was small down there and hey, it was okay. No, it was better than okay. I was cool with it.

That night, just like my girl crush Dorothy, I discovered that you can spend your whole life searching for something only to realise that what you desire is right back where you started. That's the big and small of it. From that point on I decided to embrace my boobs, whatever their size. I treated my puppies like Toto: loved them, kept them safe, stroked them on occasion, and allowed them a special kennel in my heart. And if I was ever in doubt about their brilliance, I clicked my slingbacks three times and repeated: 'There's no boobs like mine. There's no boobs like mine. There's no boobs like mine.'

CLAUDIA WINKLEMAN

'Has he latched on?'

Um, excuse me? As in, attached? As in like a latch on a door? To what exactly? Do I tie him to the bed? The curtains? Come again? Wait, don't leave. You asked me something confusing. He's small, he's perfect. Latched? Have you seen his little feet? No, don't start commenting on the weather. You seem to have uttered something important. I'm wearing bandages all over my stomach, I haven't slept in forty-eight hours, I seem to be covered in my own sick. I haven't called my friends. He's got the cutest nose and we're not sure what we're going to call him but you seem to have said something vital. Latched? Like a pincer? Hold on. Come back.

'Sorry, love. I mean latched, as in has he started drinking your milk?'

MILK? Oh, I hadn't got to that section of the 'what to do when you're pregnant' book. I see, so *that's* what they're for...

That was March 17th 2003. As a young person I had thought my boobs were for making boys fancy me, I thought that 'getting them out' was a way to attract others. I thought that having big round bouncy boobs was the actual answer. Like everyone else

I thought a Wonderbra would make all the difference. I wore big bras, red bras, skinny-strap 70s triangular bras. I flattened my breasts so I could look all fashion and cool and I threw real chicken fillets (they only really smell if you use them more than twice) under them so that I could lift and separate and make the tops all wobbly. And here I was a hundred years later and I was working out the pure and real magic of a boob.

He did latch on and he suckled and drained and squeaked and got all full up and then he would sleep on my neck like a little drunkard. Girls and boys, boobs are brilliant. Mainly because you can whip them out and feed a baby – at Café Rouge (April 2007), at the cinema (apologies to the people next to us at *Bad Santa* but I thought the snuffling didn't *totally* ruin the movie) and at the airport when you've been delayed nine hours (no, Iberia, I still haven't totally forgiven you).

Breasts are excellent. And if you don't believe me – ask my kids.

Benjamin's Breasts

BENJAMIN ZEPHANIAH

Benjamin was eleven.
One day,
As he checked out his willy,
He found he had breasts.

Benjamin was confused.
His mum told him he was a boy,
But Benjamin thought –
Only girls have titties.

Benjamin was not going to tell anybody.
He kept it a secret.
But then his breasts got bigger and bigger.
And then they got even bigger.

Benjamin was upset.
At night, before sleeping he cursed his breasts.

He thought breasts were supposed to feel nice,
But Benjamin's breasts began to hurt.

Benjamin was getting ready for football
In the school changing room,
And all the boys started to laugh at his breasts.
Benjamin began to hate his breasts.

Benjamin was sure he was becoming a girl –
A girl with some boy bits.
So Benjamin told his mum,
And she told the doctor.

Benjamin was told that he had
Gynecomastia,
'Gyne-co-whatia?' he asked.
'Such a big word,' he said.
Maybe big tits need big words, he thought.

Benjamin was excused from swimming.

Benjamin was excused from PE.

Benjamin was always excusing himself from girls.

Benjamin was always excusing himself from boys.

Benjamin was told he must have an operation.
His two breasts were sliced.

Just around the nipples,
So no one could see.

Benjamin was happy then.
He began to play football,
He began looking at girls' breasts,
But he never did learn to swim.

Benjamin was a poet,
He forgot about his breasts,
With his nipples that do nothing.
Because all men have them.

Benjamin was forty.
One day,
As he checked out his willy,
He found he had a breast.

Benjamin was unhappy.
One of his breasts had grown back.
The doctor said he had
Gynecomastia,
Again.
Just one this time.

Benjamin was told he must have an operation.
One breast was sliced.
Not around the nipple (like before).
Right around the muscle, for all to see.

Benjamin was told the doctor had no choice.
Slight complications.

Benjamin was not going to tell anybody.
He kept it a secret.

Benjamin was doing stuff
With his girlfriend. (She had breasts).
She looked at Benjamin's breast and asked –
'How did you get that scar?'
'I got it in a fight in Brixton,' said Benjamin.
'You poor thing,' she replied. 'Let me rub it.'
'It's nothing,' said Benjamin.
'You should see the other guy.'

Benjamin was wondering,
How will she feel when she reads this book?

CONTRIBUTOR BIOGRAPHIES

MAUDE APATOW

Maude Apatow is a student, actress and writer. Her work has appeared on websites such as Rookiemag, HelloGiggles, and Teen Vogue. She co-starred in the films *Knocked Up* and *This Is 40*. She is addicted to technology even though she knows it's destroying her.

EDITH BOWMAN

Edith has been at Radio 1 since 2003 and also became part of the BBC 6Music family in 2012. She's a massive music fan and fanatical gig goer. Her love and passion for film has allowed her to interview some of the biggest and most important names in film both for her radio shows and many TV specials.

Other work has included BBC's coverage of Glastonbury, T In The Park, Reading and Leeds, BBC Two's *Rough Guide to the World*, Sky One's Big Bash Comedy Awards, RISE for Channel 4 and hosting the BAFTA film awards red carpet for BBC Three for the past five years.

AMANDA BYRAM

Amanda Byram is one of Ireland's biggest exports. In 1999 she began presenting the TV3 morning show in Ireland, and she then moved to British TV, hosting *The Big Breakfast* on Channel 4. Amanda currently hosts *Total Wipeout* for CBBC, which was voted Best Gameshow at the 2010 TV Choice Awards.

2012 saw Amanda present two exciting new shows for SKY1: *The Angel* and *Don't Stop Me Now*. Amanda was also part of the team including Denise van Outen and Fearne Cotton that trekked Machu Picchu to raise awareness for Breast Cancer Care, which was documented for ITV2.

MELANIE C

Melanie C has released six solo albums. She achieved over three million album sales as well as reuniting with the Spice Girls on tour. Her theatrical debut in the West End show *Blood Brothers* was well received by critics; earning five-star reviews, a nomination for Best Actress in a Musical at the prestigious Laurence Olivier Awards, and Evening Standard Theatre Awards shortlist for the Milton Shulman Award for Outstanding Newcomer.

Whilst working on album number five, Andrew Lloyd Webber asked Melanie to join *Superstar*, the primetime TV show looking for the new Jesus to star in the UK and Ireland arena tour of *Jesus Christ Superstar*. She took the role of Mary during the arena tour alongside Tim Minchin as Judas Iscariot.

AMANDA DE CADENET

As a television personality, renowned photographer and entrepreneur, Amanda de Cadenet has evolved her body of work with an intriguing perspective and uncanny ability to render the truth across the art of storytelling.

Currently, de Cadenet can be seen as the host of *The Conversation* with Amanda de Cadenet, an ambitious series that aims to explore, nurture and empower the modern woman through thought-provoking discussions and candid interviews with notable female personalities. Beyond hosting her interview series, de Cadenet is also a renowned fashion and portrait photographer who garnered critical attention as the youngest woman to shoot a *Vogue* magazine cover. Having photographed many of the most influential figures across pop culture, de Cadenet is best known for her intimate portraits of women which reflect her eye for true beauty from behind the lens. De Cadenet's work can also be seen in the glossy pages of publications like *Harper's Bazaar*, as well as in her published ten-year compendium, *Rare Birds*, which documents and humanises her encounters with a variety of pop culture icons. Originally from the UK, de Cadenet currently resides in Los Angeles with her husband and three children.

GEMMA CAIRNEY

Gemma Cairney currently presents the weekend breakfast show on BBC Radio 1 and hosted the 2013 BBC Three live

Glastonbury coverage alongside Greg James. She presented BBC Radio 1Xtra's Breakfast Show with Trevor Nelson, for which they picked up a Silver Sony award in 2010 for Best National Breakfast Show, and her BBC Radio 1 documentary, *Bruising Silence*, won a Sony Gold Award at the Sony Radio Academy Awards 2013 for Best Documentary or Feature.

Gemma presented her first BBC Three documentary, *The Riots: The Aftermath*. Her second documentary for the channel, *Dying for Clear Skin*, highlighted the damaging effect of skin conditions and the risk of depression caused by treatment medication. Gemma was also seen on the channel's debate show, *Free Speech*, discussing issues such as benefits, body image and road safety for cyclists.

Gemma has recently finished a series on the History of Feminism for BBC Learning, which aired on BBC Two in May 2013.

SARA COX

Despite her self-confessed 'knock knees', Bolton lass Sara left school with four A-levels for a career in modelling and was soon scouted for television. Since her first TV job in 1994, she's been all over the telly – from show-jumping reality show *Only Fools And Horses* and *Top Of The Pops* to MTV and Channel 4 shows like *The Big Breakfast*. Sara joined Radio 1 in 1999 where she co-hosted the Saturday lunchtime show, followed by the Breakfast Show.

As well as raising her three children she can now be found

hosting radio shows across both Radio 1 and Radio 2 as well as popping up on various shows including *Have I Got News For You*. She also has a weekly column in the Sunday Mirror magazine, *Notebook*.

JAMES DAWSON

James Dawson is the award-nominated author of dark teen thrillers *Hollow Pike, Cruel Summer* and *Say Her Name* (Hot Key Books – May 2014). He grew up in West Yorkshire, writing imaginary episodes of Doctor Who. He later turned his talent to journalism, interviewing luminaries such as Steps and Atomic Kitten before writing a weekly serial in a Brighton newspaper.

Until recently, James worked as a teacher, specialising in PSHCE and behaviour. He is most proud of his work surrounding bullying and family diversity. His first non-fiction book, *Being a Boy* (Red Lemon Press) tackles puberty, sex and relationships in a frank and funny fashion.

James writes full time and lives in south London. In his spare time, he STILL loves Doctor Who and is a keen follower of horror films and connoisseur of pop music.

LAURA DOCKRILL

Not only author and illustrator of the *Darcy Burdock* series (Random House), *Mistakes In The Background, Ugly Shy Girl* and *Echoes* (Harper Collins), Laura also resurrects her words on the stage, performing poetry and short stories spanning festivals to bookshops; from the E4 Udderbelly, Latitude Festival and Glastonbury to the London Literary Festival, 5x15 and the BBC Proms. Named one of the top ten literary talents by *The Times* and one of the top twenty hot faces to watch by *ELLE* magazine, Laura continues to stir up the literary universe with her passionate, contemporary and imaginative way with words. She has performed her work on CBeebies, Newsnight, BBC Breakfast, Woman's Hour and each of the BBC's respective radio channels 1–6, and has been commissioned by Radio 1, 2 and 4. Laura is on the advisory panel at The Ministry Of Stories, has judged the John Betjeman Poetry Prize, is embarking on her fourth year of mentoring with the charity First Story and has been a BAFTA judge. She is currently working on her second book in the *Darcy Burdock* series, working on a film script and song writing (for others, of course!).

JENNY ECLAIR

Jenny Eclair is a stand-up comic and writer. She is the author of three novels: *Camberwell Beauty*, *Having a Lovely Time* and *Life, Death and Vanilla Slices*. She has also had a number of comedy books published including *Chin Up, Britain* and *Wendy: The Bumper Book of Fun for Women of a Certain Age*.

She pops up on the telly now and then and can sometimes be heard losing *Just a Minute* on Radio 4. Other radio writing credits include *On Baby St* and *Twilight Baby*.

She was an intrepid contestant on ITV's *I'm a Celebrity, Get Me Out of Here*, coming third in 2010.

Having appeared on the BBC's Grumpy Old Women series, she co-wrote two Grumpy Old Women Live shows, both of which went into the West End. A third live show is in production.

SOPHIE ELLIS-BEXTOR

Sophie Ellis-Bextor is a singer, songwriter and model, widely known to the British public for the past fifteen years, and has earned a place amongst pop royalty as a legendary and quintessentially British siren and starlet. Having performed throughout her childhood and teenage years, Sophie's break came with the indie rock band Theaudience in the late 90s. A couple of years later, returning to music as a solo artist, she shot straight to number one in the UK charts with her debut solo single 'Groovejet'.

Sophie has since achieved international success, releasing four top-selling albums. 2013 sees the release of her fifth album, produced by singer-songwriter Ed Harcourt. The album sees Sophie take a decidedly different musical direction.

Sophie is married to The Feeling bassist Richard Jones. The couple have three children.

CAROLINE FLACK

Caroline Flack is best known for hosting the hugely popular *Xtra Factor* alongside Olly Murs. She anchored two series of *I'm a Celebrity, Get Me Out of Here Now* and *Gladiators* for Sky One alongside Ian Wright.

A huge music fan, Caroline presented her own seven-part series for ITV2, *Indigo2*, where she interviewed some of the biggest names in the music industry. She co-hosted the Capital FM Breakfast Show and provided amusing banter as Johnny Vaughan's morning sidekick. Her love for music translated perfectly into presenting E4's Music Zones. Caroline spends her free time DJing and attending festivals. Originally from Norfolk, Caroline trained as an actress and dancer before focusing her energies on TV presenting.

KRISTIN HALLENGA

Kristin Hallenga started CoppaFeel! with her twin sister Maren one month after her breast cancer diagnosis at 23. Discovering a lump in her boob in June 2008, Kris went to her GP, only to be sent away. Within weeks Kris was appearing on TV and in national press sharing her story and raising money for a campaign that would prove to save lives and keep other young people from the same fate as hers. She won the Pride of Britain award with a Downing Street reception. After a secondary breast cancer diagnosis, Kris is not cancer free – and perhaps never will be. Whenever she's not in the presence of doctors, she's pouring her heart and soul into making a success of CoppaFeel!, not only refusing to let cancer wreck her party, but refusing to let it ruin yours too. To find out more go to www.coppafeel.org.

CHERRY HEALEY

Best known for her hugely successful BBC Three documentaries, Cherry is insightful, witty, challenging and compassionate about the subjects she covers, with a genuine desire to give voice to the true character of the contributors she encounters. Cherry's documentaries for BBC Three include *Cherry Has a Baby*, *Cherry Goes Dating* and *Cherry Gets Married* (2010), *Is Breast Best?* (2011), a six-part series in 2012, *Cherry Healey: How to Get a Life*, and a second six-part series in 2013, *The Year of Making Love*.

With a Degree in Drama Education/Drama for Social Change from Central School of Speech and Drama, Cherry has a particular interest in women's ever-changing roles in society – giving light to new cultural trends in a (sometimes painfully!) honest and entertaining way. Whilst studying, she set up a company teaching dance to kids at risk of exclusion in community centres. She is a drama, hip-hop and break-dance teacher, having herself competed in several national competitions (and has also been a backing dancer for the infamous Ice T!). Cherry has also written for several publications including *Grazia*, *You Me Baby* magazine, and Cellardoor online, and has a unique and funny style that appeals to a wide audience.

WILL HILL

Will Hill is the author of the bestselling *Department 19* series, and has contributed short stories and novellas to a number of award-nominated anthologies. He was a juror for the inaugural Hot Key Books Young Writers Prize and the 2013 Kitschies Awards.

He grew up in the north-east of England and worked as a bartender, a bookseller, and a door-to-door charity worker in California before quitting a job in publishing to write full time. He lives in east London with his girlfriend.

RUFUS HOUND

Rufus Hound is a comedian, presenter and actor. You may have seen him in *The Wedding Video*, winning *Let's Dance for Sport Relief* dressed up as Cheryl Cole or as the eponymous hero of CBBC's *Hounded*. He hosts Radio 4's Sony Award-winning *My Teenage Diary* and most recently took over as Francis Henshall in The National Theatre's *One Man, Two Guvnors*. Of course, it may be equally true that you have no idea who he is, and no one would blame you for that.

AMY HUBERMAN

Amy Huberman was born in Dublin, and is a graduate of UCD and the Dublin Institute of Technology. She is an actress and a novelist.

She made her first appearance on Irish television in the RTE drama *On Home Ground* and went on to star in *The Clinic* (RTE) for which she was nominated as Best Supporting Actress at the IFTA Awards in 2009. Amy has also appeared in several films including *A Film With Me In It* opposite Dylan Moran and Mark Doherty, *Redux* directed by P.J. Dillon, and *Stella Days* starring Martin Sheen. She has also appeared in the TV comedy sketch show *Your Bad Self* for RTE, and most recently took the female lead in two series of Comedy Central's popular sitcom *Threesome*.

Amy has also written two bestselling novels, *Hello Heartbreak* (Penguin, 2009) and *I Wished For You* (Penguin, 2012).

JAMEELA JAMIL

Jameela Jamil recently took on Radio 1's The Official Chart Show, making her the first female presenter to host the show solo since its inception. Jameela began her presenting career in 2008 on the E4 Music Zone. In 2012 she featured in E4's cult series, *Playing It Straight*. Jameela launched her first clothing range, JAM by Jameela Jamil, in 2012 with very.co.uk, and she was nominated for columnist of the year at both the prestigious PPA Awards and the BSME Awards for her monthly column in *Company* magazine. Jameela has also fronted a TV advertising campaign for international make-up brand Maybelline and has done fashion shoots with magazines including American and UK *Vogue*, *InStyle* and *Esquire*.

MAUREEN JOHNSON

Maureen Johnson was recently crowned the 2012 Queen of Teen in the UK – but, as it turns out, she is American. She was born in Philadelphia, Pennsylvania, during a massive snowstorm. After a little dalliance with astronomy (she had a glow in the dark star chart) and archaeology (she had a little shovel), Maureen declared her intention to become a writer at the age of eight or nine or so. She is the *New York Times* bestselling author of ten YA novels (including *Suite Scarlett, Scarlett Fever, 13 Little Blue Envelopes, The Name of the Star*, and *The Madness Underneath*). She has also done many collaborative works, such as *Let It Snow* (with John Green and Lauren Myracle), and *The Bane Chronicles* (with Cassandra Clare and Sarah Rees Brennan). She writes frequently on the subject of Young Adult literature for many publications, and is well known for her online presence on Twitter (@ maureenjohnson). Maureen lives in New York, and online on Twitter (or at www.maureenjohnbooks.com). She's not giving that crown back.

ALEX JONES

Alex is the co-host of the BBC's flagship magazine programme *The One Show* alongside Matt Baker and Chris Evans. Alex has also appeared as a panellist on *8 Out of 10 Cats* and co-presented *Let's Dance for Comic Relief* for the third year running. In 2011 she was a semi-finalist on *Strictly Come*

Dancing, and 2012 saw Alex dance at Buckingham Palace on *The One Show*.

A fluent Welsh speaker, Alex's television career began working for Welsh Channel S4C, and she went on to present a variety of shows for the channel. In 2009 Alex took part in *The Magnificent Seven*, a BAFTA-winning series which saw seven celebrities travel to a ranch in Arizona to learn how to become cowboys. Whilst in the Wild West she recorded a spin-off children's series called *Alex and the Cowboys*, also for S4C. Alex went on to present BBC Wales' contribution to the *Children in Need* network programme from the Millennium Stadium.

In Summer 2010, Alex landed *The One Show* role and she hasn't looked back since. She presents the daily magazine show from London and has become a mainstay on the channel, presenting Eurovision results and *Let's Dance for Comic Relief* for BBC One.

MARIAN KEYES

Marian Keyes is a hugely successful Irish novelist, born in Limerick in 1963. She was brought up in a home where a lot of oral storytelling went on; however she studied law and accountancy. She finally started writing short stories in 1993 'out of the blue'. Marian is now published in thirty-three languages and has written articles for various magazines and other publications. Her novel *Anybody Out There* won the British Book Awards award for popular fiction and the inaugural Melissa Nathan prize for Comedy Romance. *This Charming Man* won the Irish Book award for popular fiction. In 2012, she published *Saved by Cake*, which combines recipes with autobiography, novel *The Mystery of Mercy Close* and ebook short, *Mammy Walsh's A–Z of the Walsh Family*.

ANNIE MACMANUS

Having left her home town of Dublin at 17, Radio 1's Queen of Dance Annie Mac has spent the last decade carving out a career as a tastemaker, talent-finder and international DJ.

Annie currently hosts the prestigious Friday night 7–9pm slot on Radio 1, helping the nation to start the weekend. She also presents the 10pm–midnight Radio 1 show on Sunday evenings.

She is also known for championing cutting-edge new artists and DJs through her own brand 'Annie Mac Presents'.

AMP, which started out as a club night at Fabric in London, now hosts stellar line-ups personally curated by Annie on international stages, tents at major festivals and club nights throughout the UK. The Annie Mac Presents compilation is one of the biggest albums in the dance music calendar each year.

Her TV work has included presenting the music series *Sound* for BBC Two as well as fronting the iTunes Festival and Ibiza Rocks for Channel 4.

SARRA MANNING

Sarra Manning has been a fashion, lifestyle and entertainment journalist for over fifteen years. Her writing career started on the music paper *Melody Maker* and involved a long stint on the legendary teen mag *J17*. She then worked on the launch of and edited *Elle Girl* and *What To Wear*, as well as consulting on a number of magazines including *The Face*, *Look* and *More*. Sarra also writes for *Grazia*, *Red*, *The Guardian*, *Stylist*, *Fabulous*, *Stella*, *You Magazine*, and *InStyle*.

Her first adult novel, *Unsticky*, was *Heat* magazine's book of the week. Her other adult novels are *You Don't Have To Say You Love Me* and *Nine Uses For An Ex-Boyfriend*. Sarra is also the queen of UK YA fiction. Her bestselling teen novels include *Adorkable*, *Guitar Girl*, *Let's Get Lost* and the iconic *Diary Of A Crush* trilogy. Sarra has both an adult novel *It Felt Like A Kiss* and a YA title, *The Worst Girlfriend In The World* set for publication in 2014.

Sarra lives in North London with her beloved Staffordshire Bull Terrier, Miss Betsy, and prides herself on her unique ability to accessorise.

DAVINA MCCALL

Davina McCall was born in London in 1967 and currently hosts hit series *The Million Pound Drop*, *Long Lost Family* and *Stepping Out*. In addition, Davina has been the face (and hair) for the L'Oréal brands Garnier and Nutrisse for the past ten years and is currently the UK's Number 1 fitness DVD franchise. Davina also starred in the BBC documentary *Let's Talk Sex*, looking at how sex education is taught in Britain, and hosted all eleven series of *Big Brother* for Channel 4.

In October 2012, Davina, along with Gwyneth Paltrow, Alan Carr, Dr Christian and Cancer Research UK, launched the UK's version of the epic US charity fundraising show Stand Up to Cancer, hosting over six hours of TV for Channel 4 and raising £7million . . . and counting! She is also an active supporter and campaigner for the charities Focus 12 and Action Medical Research.

SARAH MILLICAN

Sarah Millican has fast established herself as a household name since winning the 2008 if.comedy Best Newcomer Award (formerly the Perrier Award) for her debut solo stand-up show at the Edinburgh Fringe Festival.

Crowned The People's Choice: Queen of Comedy at the 2011 British Comedy Awards, Sarah has completed two sell-out national tours, playing to over 200,000 people, and she will embark on her third tour in the autumn of 2013, performing over 140 dates across the UK. Sarah's debut DVD, *Chatterbox Live*, became the biggest selling stand-up DVD by a female comedian of all time.

This year, Sarah was nominated for a BAFTA for Best Entertainment Performance for her own series on BBC Two, *The Sarah Millican Television Programme*. The show combines stand-up inspired by what she has seen on TV as well as unique interviews with television stars who have impressed her. Filming has just wrapped on the third series. Other TV appearances include *QI*, *Live at the Apollo*, *Michael McIntyre's Comedy Roadshow* and *The Graham Norton Show*.

SIMITCHELL

SiMitchell is a professional artist from the UK. He loves cartoons, punk music, his lady and his cat! He also loves to draw and spray paint silly things. He has been producing artwork for clients such as Green Day, The Midnight Beast, Mcfly, E4 and RockSound among many many others.

LEE MONROE

Lee Monroe was born in London, but spent a short time living by the sea with her family when she was a teenager. She moved back to the heart of the city as soon as she could, and now lives in London.

Lee was an obsessive reader as a child, and still is. She works in publishing and has written fiction for children and adults, including a paranormal trilogy under her own name for young adults, called Dark Heart, and more recently a contemporary romance called *Love is a Number*.

CAITLIN MORAN

Caitlin Moran wrote her first novel, *The Chronicles of Narmo*, at the age of fifteen. At sixteen she joined music weekly *Melody Maker*, and at eighteen briefly presented the pop show *Naked City* on Channel 4. She wrote as columnist on *The Times* – both as a TV critic and also in the most-read part of the paper, the satirical celebrity column 'Celebrity Watch' – winning the British Press Awards' Columnist of The Year award in 2010 and Critic and Interviewer of the Year in 2011.

The eldest of eight children, home-educated in a council house in Wolverhampton, Caitlin read lots of books about feminism. Caitlin isn't really her name. She was christened 'Catherine'. But she saw 'Caitlin' in a Jilly Cooper novel when she was thirteen and thought it looked exciting. That's why she pronounces it incorrectly: 'Catlin'. It causes trouble for everyone.

PATRICK NESS

Born in America, Patrick Ness now lives in London. He is the author of seven novels, a short story collection, varied journalism and radio plays. You might have heard of his trilogy *Chaos Walking*, his latest book for adults *The Crane Wife*, which came out earlier this year, or even *A Monster Calls*, which became the first book ever to win both the Kate Greenaway and Carnegie Medals in 2012. His books are published in over twenty languages and among others Patrick has won the Carnegie Medal twice, the Guardian Children's Fiction Prize, the Costa Children's Book Award and the Red House Children's Book Award. Watch out for his daring new YA novel *More Than This*, forthcoming later this year from Walker Books.

ERIN O'CONNOR

Erin O'Connor was born in 1978 in Walsall. Erin's big break came during a shoot in Brazil, with photographer David Sims and hairdresser Guido, when she decided to get her hair cut off. She first modelled for Juergen Teller in a 1996 issue of *i-D* and she was described as 'freak chic' – but went on to model for most of the luxury brands, top photographers, always at couture and, in 2007, the revamped Marks & Spencer. Swan-like, porcelain-skinned, hard-working, and tall (6ft 4in in heels). 'She isn't only a model,' Jean Paul Gaultier famously raved, 'she is quite art. She is like theatre. She is extraordinary inspiration. I should love to be with her every day.'

The illustrator David Downtown made her his muse.

CHRIS O'DOWD

Chris O'Dowd is from Roscommon, Ireland. He studied politics at Dublin University before training at LAMDA.Chris is well known for his starring role in *Bridesmaids* opposite Kristen Wiig and Maya Rudolph. For his role in the film, Chris was nominated for a BAFTA 'Rising Star Award', a Screen Actor's Guild Award for 'Outstanding Performance by a Cast in a Motion Picture' and won the Irish Film and Television Award for 'Best Supporting Actor – Film'. Chris has also recently starred in Wayne Blair's *The Sapphires*, Judd Apatow's *This Is 40* and Lena Dunham's HBO series *Girls*, and is currently starring in the hit HBO series *Family Tree*.

Chris wrote and produced an award-winning TV series based on his childhood titled *Moone Boy*. Having premiered on Sky One in the UK and Hulu, the show has been picked up for a third season, and in addition to writing and producing, Chris will direct all the upcoming episodes. Chris's other upcoming features include John Michael McDonagh's *Calvary* opposite Kelly Reilly and Brendan Gleeson and James Griffiths' *Cuban Fury* opposite Nick Frost and Rashida Jones.

Chris's television credits include starring in the cult comedy series *The It Crowd* for Channel 4 and the critically acclaimed series *Crimson Petal & The White* for the BBC.

DERMOT O'LEARY

Dermot O'Leary spends his Saturday nights hosting ITV1's *The X Factor* and, to the sometime annoyance of his family, who occasionally like to see him on a weekend, has done since 2007. His specialist subjects include scalding judges, hugging, and the occasional dance. He hosted *The X Factor* following his success as host of *Big Brother's Little Brother* on E4. Dermot established the hugely successful T4 for Channel 4.

He spends his Saturday afternoons presenting *The Dermot O'Leary Show* on BBC Radio 2 (a mix of indie and interviews), winning the Sony Radio Award for The Best Music Programme in 2008, 2010 and recently in 2013.

2010 saw Dermot chairing BBC Three political debate *First Time Voters Question Time* and *Dermot Meets*, where he interviewed David Cameron, Gordon Brown and Nick Clegg.

He owns his own production company (Ora et Labora), is a very active partner in his fish restaurant in Brighton (Fishy Fishy), and is a keen Arsenal fan . . . for his sins in a previous life.

DAWN O'PORTER

Dawn O'Porter is a broadcaster and print journalist who lives in London with her husband Chris, cat Lilu and dog Potato. She has made numerous documentaries about all sorts of things, including polygamy, childbirth, geishas, body image, breast cancer and even the movie *Dirty Dancing*.

Dawn has written for many UK newspapers and magazines including *Grazia* and *Stylist* and she is currently a columnist for *Glamour* magazine. Her first fictional novel, *Paper Aeroplanes*, was published by Hot Key Books in 2013. Although Dawn lives in London she spends a lot of time in LA and travels a lot. She is obsessed with cats, mad about dogs, has an addiction to vintage dresses and she loves food.

THE VAGENDA

Feminist writers Rhiannon Lucy Cosslett and Holly Baxter founded the online magazine The Vagenda in January 2012. Since then, The Vagenda has published bylined, anonymous and editorial articles on topics ranging from cosmetic surgery and pop songs, to the 'cupcake conspiracy' and Republicans. Humorous and topical with a searing, critical streak, The Vagenda exposes the mainstream female press for its insidious elements – and its frequent ridiculousness.

VICTORIA WHITE

Victoria White is the editor of young women's fashion magazine, *Company*. She has won awards for doing this. It is a dream job. She gets to see all the clothes the high street has to offer six months before they go into store. She gets to go to cool music events and found herself backstage with One Direction when they won a BRIT Award. She's been a guest judge on seven series of *Britain and Ireland's Next Top Model* (which is where she first met Dawn O'Porter seven years ago – long story). Oh, and this year she played herself in two episodes of *Hollyoaks* (badly). She tweets and instagrams as @companyedvic and she has her own blog, www.weboughtafrenchhouse.com about her 'other' life renovating property in south-west France. She has two boys, Arthur, aged ten and Sebastian, aged six. They all live with her husband Peter in a large, in need of renovation, house in south-east

London. So at weekends, when not watching *Million Pound Drop* or shopping at Westfield Stratford, she can be found painting and decorating. She is really quite tired.

LAURA WHITMORE

Laura Whitmore is one of the most in-demand young presenters currently working in television. Combining her love of music, people and fashion, she has covered all the major festivals both here and internationally and interviewed the likes of Coldplay, Justin Bieber and more recently Michael Caine. Laura's recent TV credits include: *I'm A Celebrity, Get Me Out Of Here* 2011, The Brits 2012 (ITV2), MTV European Music Awards 2012.

Laura has always been a huge music fan and loves to get behind the decks to DJ whenever possible. She's brought her rock 'n' roll set to a number of high-end fashion, branded and international events.

MATT WHYMAN

Matt Whyman is the bestselling author of several novels and comic memoirs. His books include *Pig in the Middle, Walking with Sausage Dogs, Boy Kills Man* and *The Savages*. Matt is married with four children and lives in West Sussex.

LARA WILLIAMSON

Lara Williamson was born and studied in Northern Ireland. After graduating with a BA (Hons) in Fashion Design she moved to London and was Beauty Editor for *J17* where she wrote and styled shoots, both in Britain and foreign locations.

Lara won The Jasmine Awards for Best Article in a Youth Title, and received an Honorary Mention in *Undiscovered Voices 2012*. Lara lives in London with her family.

CLAUDIA WINKLEMAN

Claudia Winkleman works in television and radio. She talks mostly about films, books, the foxtrot and theatre. She has three children and is fond of owls.

BENJAMIN ZEPHANIAH

Benjamin Zephaniah was born in Birmingham, England. He spent some of his early years in Jamaica, his parents' homeland, where he was strongly influenced by Jamaican folk music. Back in England, he had a difficult school life. He enrolled in adult education to learn how to read and write and then discovered he was dyslexic.

Since the age of twenty-two, he's been writing, publishing and mostly 'performing' his poetry in tours all over the world. Zephaniah writes gritty, realistic novels about the lives of teenagers, aimed at adults as much as they are at teenagers. He believes that for the most part teenagers know what they are going through, but adults need reminding; they have short memories. He now devotes much of his time to visiting schools, prisons, universities and teacher training centres. Zephaniah believes that working with human rights groups, animal rights groups and other political organisations means that he will never lack subject matter.

ABOUT THE CHARITIES

BREAST CANCER
BREAKTHROUGH

Breakthrough Breast Cancer is the UK's leading charity dedicated to stopping women dying from breast cancer through improving early diagnosis, developing new treatments and preventing all types of the disease.

Breakthrough Breast Cancer set up a research centre dedicated to breast cancer when no other existed in Europe. Today, we fund 25% of the breast cancer research in the UK as well as campaigning to ensure survival rates are among the best in the world.

The need for Breakthrough Breast Cancer's work has never been greater. Breast cancer affects more women every year and is still the most commonly diagnosed cancer in the UK.

Breakthrough Breast Cancer wants all women to be breast aware. Our award-winning Touch Look Check (TLC) campaign teaches women the common signs and symptoms of breast cancer that they must look out for, as the earlier breast cancer is found the better the chances of beating it.

Find out more at www.breakthrough.org.uk or @BreakthroughBC

We at Breast Cancer Care are incredibly grateful to Dawn for all her fantastic support over the years. She has taken part in our nationwide fundraising campaign Pink Fridays, appeared on Channel 4's Million Pound Drop Live, and got on her bike to cycle from London to Paris to raise money for our services. Dawn also gathered together a host of comedians and performers to create the inaugural Best Friends Ball in September 2013. Dawn's support has helped us continue our essential work for the nearly 50,000 people diagnosed with breast cancer each year in the UK. Breast Cancer Care is the only specialist breast cancer support charity working throughout the UK. Through our face-to-face, phone and online services we are able to provide direct support to the millions of women and their families who face the devastating physical and emotional impact of living with breast cancer, every day. Visit www.breastcancercare.org.uk or call our free helpline on 0808 800 6000.

CoppaFeel! is on a mission to stamp out late detection and diagnosis of breast cancer by ensuring that you know the signs and symptoms of breast cancer, know what your boobs look and feel like normally, check your boobs regularly throughout your lifetime and have the confidence to seek medical referral if you detect any changes. We want to make this as habitual as making a cup of tea because it could just save your life. So, isn't it time you checked your boobs?

www.coppafeel.org

Over 49,000 women and 400 men are diagnosed
with breast cancer each year in the UK.

Knowing the signs and symptoms of breast cancer and
what your boobs look and feel like normally could save
your life. Start the habit of a lifetime today. The earlier
breast cancer is diagnosed, the easier it is to treat.

Know your boobs!

Why?

Why not? You feel your boobs anyway, so get to know them
a little better. That way, you'll spot any problems faster than
you can say 'CoppaFeel!'

What?

You need to know what it is you're looking and feeling for.
Learn and familiarise yourself with the possible signs and
symptoms, but remember that there can be many reasons
for changes in the breast which are harmless.

When?

Whenever. There is no good or bad time for boob time.
Perhaps get your partner to lend you a hand and remind
yourself to cop a feel regularly. We can remind you, by the
way, with our handy iCoppaFeel! app.

Where?

Wherever. At the bus stop? On top of a mountain? In the shower perhaps. Find a place for boob time in your routine and try to keep it up.

Who?

The person you need to see if you find anything unusual is your GP. Share your worries and remember, you know your boobs better than anyone and because you've copped a feel regularly, you know your boobs better than your GP and will be in a better position to tell them what is normal for you.

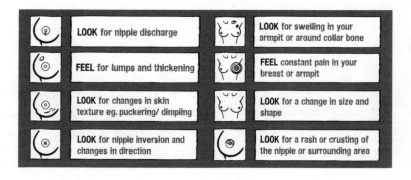

LOOK for nipple discharge

LOOK for swelling in your armpit or around collar bone

FEEL for lumps and thickening

FEEL constant pain in your breast or armpit

LOOK for changes in skin texture eg. puckering/ dimpling

LOOK for a change in size and shape

LOOK for nipple inversion and changes in direction

LOOK for a rash or crusting of the nipple or surrounding area

From Dawn O'Porter

I just wanted to say a huge personal thank you to everyone who contributed to this book. It's always hard to ask very busy people to offer their time for free, and I have been amazed by the generosity and honesty of you all. This book is brilliant, and that is all down to how willing you all were to write about a subject as close to all of our hearts as breast cancer. From Maude Apatow's mind-blowing account of a teenager's issues with her own breasts, to Laura Dockrill's hilarious poem and to Gemma Cairney's sore nipple, I love each and every one of your stories, poems and personal triumphs. From myself and all the boobies that this book helps, thank you. Thank you so, so much!

Now, go tweet the shit out of it!

Hot Key Books would like to give particular thanks to each of the talented contributors to this special anthology, and big thanks to Dawn O'Porter for putting The Booby Trap together with such style and generosity.

Contributors

Maude Apatow, 'I am Fifteen, and Have Nothing Figured Out' © Maude Apatow 2013

Holly Baxter, 'Beauty and the B(r)easts © Holly Baxter 2013

Edith Bowman © Edith Bowman 2013

Amanda Byram © Amanda Byram 2013

Melanie C © Melanie C 2013

Amanda de Cadenet © Amanda de Cadenet 2013

Gemma Cairney, 'The NBB' © Gemma Cairney 2013

Rhiannon Lucy Cosslett, 'Boob Envy' © Rhiannon Lucy Cosslett, 2013

Sara Cox © Sara Cox 2013

James Dawson, 'Diary of a Boob Job' © James Dawson 2013

Laura Dockrill, 'A Diamond-Encrusted Bubble-Gum-Flavoured Speckled Glittered Brightly Coloured Erotic Eye-Wateringly Bouncy yet Sensible, Comfortable Hammock (with pockets) © Laura Dockrill 2013

Jenny Eclair © Jenny Eclair 2013

Sophie Ellis-Bextor © Sophie Ellis-Bextor 2013

Caroline Flack © Caroline Flack 2013

Kristin Hallenga © Kristin Hallenga 2013

Cherry Healey © Cherry Healey © 2013

Will Hill, 'Ben Harris and the Orbs of Power' © Will Hill 2013

Hot Key Books will pay 33.33p per book sold to Breakthrough Promotions Ltd which pays all its taxable profits to Breakthrough Breast Cancer, a registered charity in England and Wales (1062636) and Scotland (SC039058) under the Gift Aid scheme.

Hot Key Books will pay 33.33p per book sold to Breast Cancer Care (Registered charity in England and Wales 1017658, and Scotland SC038104).

Hot Key Books will pay 33.33p per book sold to CoppaFeel! (Registered charity in England and Wales 1132366).